The Secrets He Keeps

Peril & Persuasion

Amy Sandas

Published by Amy Sandas, 2021.

This is a work of fiction. Similarities to real people, places, or events are entirely coincidental.

THE SECRETS HE KEEPS

First edition. January 19, 2021.

Copyright © 2021 Amy Sandas.

Written by Amy Sandas.

This one is for all the boss babes. May you continue to reign over your domain with grace, wisdom, and brazen fearlessness.

Chapter One

London, December 1817

Callista Hale stepped gracefully from her stylish barouche to the cobblestone street in Soho. A winter gale kicked up and swirled around her feet, sending gusts of icy air up her skirts. Ignoring the cold, she peered through the black netting of her hat, which had been drawn down to conceal her features, and assessed the building in front of her.

It was not as grand as she'd expected.

Her own establishment near St. James was a veritable mansion built of red brick with ivy crawling up one wall, black shutters on every window, and a black-painted door possessing a gleaming brass knocker in the shape of a dragon's head. This place was nearly its exactly opposite. Built in the romantic neo-classical style, it was three stories high but remained rather modest in size. It was all white with solid white pillars framing the entrance and marble steps that led up to double doors painted a conservative navy blue.

Smoothing her hands over the fur-lined black velvet of her winter pelisse, she started forward. Anyone observing would have seen a mysterious woman of obvious wealth and consequence. They'd have no idea the black veil concealed a shrewd and focused gaze. Or that such graceful, languid steps were grounded in determination and ire.

Because she was about to infiltrate the enemy's lair.

Whispers and rumors about London's newest gentleman's club had been flying about town for months. At first, Callista had brushed off the news of a new place opening up. No club, brothel, or otherwise had ever been able to compete with Pendragon's Pleasure House.

Callista should have easily been able to put any possible concerns about the new gentleman's club to rest. And she would have, if she hadn't started to notice that for all the talk it inspired, no one really seemed to know exactly what went on behind the establishment's blue doors.

Even after months of using her rather extensive resources to learn more about the establishment in Soho, Callista had confirmed very little that proved to be useful or concrete beyond the fact that the place was owned and operated by one Erik Maxwell of unknown origins. And for a woman who'd been the primary custodian for the sexual secrets of England's most prominent aristocrats, politicians, and businessmen for more than a decade, the lack of information was infuriating.

She did not tolerate competition, and though she doubted this new club could possibly be considered as such, she'd had enough with the bloody mystery. The fact that the club catered to the same pool of extremely wealthy and influential gentlemen as Pendragon's was enough to place the establishment in her line of fire. It was time to discover exactly what secrets Maxwell's contained. Personally.

As she ascended the pristine steps to the front doors, she put an extra sway in her hips and curved her reddened lips. Poor Mr. Maxwell had no idea what he was up against.

Lifting a hand gloved in the finest black leather, she ignored the gleaming gold knocker to rap her knuckles smartly on the wood. The door opened immediately to reveal a man who possessed the appearance and manner of an aged butler. Stiff spine, hooked nose, disapproving glare and all.

"May I help you, madam?"

Though the pompous servant was not what she'd expected, she replied with smooth command. "I desire an audience with the proprietor of this establishment."

"Do you have an appointment?"

She laughed—a rich, husky, sensual sound. Assuming the man would continue his butler charade and refrain from physically stopping her, she swept past him into the building and began unbuttoning her pelisse. Though she probably shouldn't have been, she was surprised to see that the attempt at mimicking an aristocratic home had not been limited to the doorman. The entryway was set up to give a visitor the impression they were entering a gentleman's townhouse rather than a high-class brothel.

"Pardon me, madam, but all visitations are by appointment only."

Lifting the small velvet reticule looped over her wrist, she slipped her hand in to withdraw a calling card printed in red ink on black. With a graceful turn of her elbow, she handed the card to the butler. "Take this to your master. He'll receive me. With pleasure, I'm sure."

Then she turned and strode toward one of the open doors leading off the hall. She had no doubt the butler would do as she said and even less doubt the man she wished to speak with would see her immediately upon receiving her card. She had only about five minutes or so to snoop around a bit.

As she listened to the butler's steps crossing the gleaming marble floor behind her, she entered what proved to be a small library.

She scoffed. Who the hell featured a library in a blasted brothel?

Although she had one at Pendragon's, it was for her own personal use. Men did not come to a pleasure house to read. Yet this was clearly intended for the club's guests. For a moment, she wondered if she had the wrong address.

But her information had been confirmed. This *was* definitely Maxwell's.

The floor was covered in thick Persian rugs and a grand fireplace occupied nearly the entire wall to her right. Leather chairs and sofas offered comfortable seating while books lined the opposite wall from floor to ceiling. The room felt like a quiet and studious sanctuary.

Callista laughed as she removed her pelisse and draped it over her arm. It was all so...lord-of-the-manor. So pretentious and arrogant and *aristocratic*.

She was all about discretion and keeping the specific activities at her brothel private and protected for the sake of her patrons. But no one walked into her place and didn't immediately know it existed for the expression and enjoyment of sin, sex, and all manners of wickedness. There was no shame in it.

Annoyance seared her blood as she looked about the room, judging it harshly for its attempt at elevating the establishment above its purpose. It was a brothel. Nothing more. One of many that had tried to pilfer some of her elite clientele. All the others eventually perished from a failure to replicate the kind of service Pendragon's provided.

This place would do the same.

"Pardon, madam," the butler intoned from the doorway. "Mr. Maxwell will see you. This way, if you please."

Callista smiled beneath her veil. Of course the man would see her. No one could resist an audience with Madam Pendragon, a woman celebrated throughout London for being the owner and proprietor of the most elite and fashionable brothel in all of England. It was a position she had no intention of relinquishing any time soon.

The butler led her up the wide mahogany staircase to a spacious landing on the second floor. From there, two hallways extended in opposite directions. Both were lit by elegant gas lamps and were lushly carpeted in more Persian rugs.

She paused to see which hallway the butler would lead her down and was momentarily surprised when he continued straight forward instead. The wall across from the landing displayed an elaborate carved relief depicting a scene of woodland stags and other small forest creatures.

Callista tilted her head as she studied the piece. Almost all of the artwork within Pendragon's depicted Grecian themes of sexual congress—nymphs and satyrs, Zeus in his many forms with his many conquests. But this large bit of art was not the slightest bit sexual. It really was just a woodland scene.

The butler stepped toward the carved relief to press two fingertips against a knot carved into the image of a gnarled oak tree. There was a near silent click and then the entire wall panel gently swung open to reveal a short hallway and another staircase.

Callista's lips twisted with reluctant appreciation. *Finally, a little drama!*

But why would the club's proprietor have her brought up to what were obviously his private quarters when he could just as easily have come down to meet her in one of the common rooms? At Pendragon's, she had a special apartment of rooms that were designed to appear as her private suite, though it was nothing more than an illusion to make the clients she received there feel important and cherished.

It made no sense, however, to go through the trouble of concealing the entrance to your personal rooms in such a way if you were going to reveal them to your visitors. Unless, he was trying to demonstrate that although he kept such things from his patrons' knowledge, he saw her differently. Was it a way of treating her as colleague rather than guest or rival?

It suggested he knew exactly what he was doing. This man might prove to be a better adversary than she'd expected. A thrill of particular poignancy danced across her nape and she almost wished it were true. Ultimately, however, no man had ever proven himself to be equal to her in cleverness or ambition. She always won in the end.

At the top of the secret stairway, the butler activated another hidden latch and the wall in front of them opened to a better-lit hallway. The third floor was as richly decorated and conservatively styled as the lower levels. It appeared the whole place was a study in aristocratic, gentlemanly décor. Cultured, generic, and—aside from the secret stairway—rather boring.

Stopping in front of an open room, the butler clicked his heels and gestured stoically for her to enter.

Pompous.

With a roll of her eyes, she handed the servant her pelisse before sweeping past him in a subtle rustle of skirts. She sensed rather than heard him close the door behind her as she found herself in a spacious room dimly lit by candles. Instead of thick carpets underfoot, the floor was a warm, gleaming wood that reflected the dancing firelight from the carved stone hearth. The only furniture in the rather Spartan space was the wide, imposing desk placed in front of the fireplace and the two tall wingback chairs that faced it.

Upon her entrance, the man seated behind the desk rose to his feet. With the fire glowing behind him, she was able to discern that he was a tall man, dressed in dark clothing, with broad shoulders and a trim torso. It was a pleasingly masculine form suggestive of strength and vigor. But Callista had a gift for seeing men with more than her eyes. She could often sense things about them—fears, worries, vulnerabilities, and desires—before they could put them into words. She prided herself on being able to understand the things men preferred to keep buried deep inside.

Already, she could feel the quiet restraint in this one. Though he'd only moved to stand, a steady force emanated from him. As though he could leap into action at any moment but chose quite deliberately not to. That he hadn't spoken yet suggested he was accustomed to taking his time, allowing things to fall into place as they would before taking command. And he would try to take command. That was evident as well. This was a man who embraced his power quietly but with definite assurance.

But he'd never come up against anyone like her before.

As she strode across the rather cavernous room, Callista knew very well that although he was in deep shadow, she was cast in a fiery light. Her favorite kind. Her black brocade gown would reflect some of the flickering glow while retaining its mysterious darkness, showing off the deep curves of her figure and accenting the sensual movement of her body. Her fair hair would ignite with the light of the flames while her veil would keep her face concealed until she chose to reveal it. Though he couldn't see it, her gaze remained sharply trained upon the infamously secretive man who'd become her temporary rival.

Reaching the space between the two wingback chairs, she paused to give a disdainful tilt of her head.

Mr. Erik Maxwell, who no one in London had heard of prior to his arrival nearly eight months ago, lifted his hand in a small but definitive gesture. "Please have a seat, madam. It is my honor to receive you."

The words were formed in a slight, indiscernible accent with a voice that made her think of fine cigars and even finer brandy. Decadent, rich, and masculine, with just the slightest hint of roughness around the edges. Rolled together with understated but undeniable command and confidence.

Goose bumps—delicate and tingling—spread across her skin. She didn't enjoy the feeling.

Sweeping forward, she lowered herself into one of the chairs. The tall, straight back did not prevent her from reclining with the sensual grace she was famous for. From her new angle in the chair, she was able to discern more details of the man's face when she glanced up at him.

He looked to be close to fifty in age, though a very virile, well-maintained fifty, to be sure. His hair—dark and liberally laced with silver—was brushed back from a square forehead. Deep-set eyes of an indiscernible color addressed her with keen attention from behind square spectacles. Strong cheekbones, an angled jaw currently shadowed with a day's growth of salt-and-pepper beard, and a wide sensual mouth.

He was undoubtedly the most distinguished-looking sex proprietor she'd ever seen. A gentleman pimp? The thought made her lips curl.

She replied to his greeting in a smooth, unhurried tone, "I hope my unexpected visit isn't too much of an imposition."

By the subtle arch of his dark, slashing brow, she knew they were both aware that imposing was her exact intention. When she saw the twitch of a smile at the corner of his mouth, her blood heated with a sensation she hadn't felt in a very long time.

Desire. Attraction. *Lust*.

Dammit. Of course her long-dormant libido would choose now to reignite. But she had never been subservient to her more base desires and she quickly buried the unwanted physical reaction.

"You may feel free to impose upon me anytime, madam," he said as he reclaimed his seat.

His tone was sincere. The man was smooth.

Shifting in the chair, she slowly lifted the veil from her face. "Well, I do not expect my purpose to require more than one." Meeting his eyes without the black netting filtering her view proved more unsettling than she'd expected. The man had a poignant gaze. "I shall assume you are an intelligent man and that you know why I'm here."

He lowered his chin and the look he gave her then would have made her pulse flutter if she had been a weaker woman. "I would never presume to know a woman's mind."

"Intelligent, indeed."

He flashed his teeth in a brief smile. "Tell me what you need of me and I shall endeavor to please you."

She ignored the tightness his words and voice and eyes created low in her body. A sharp edge entered her voice as she replied with a practiced smile. "What would please me, Mr. Maxwell, is your exodus from London."

Her declaration did not appear to surprise him. Leaning back in his chair, he linked his fingers over his abdomen and returned her steady stare. The curve of his mouth was undeniable, as was the lowered, more intimate tone of his voice as he replied. "It appears you are everything you've been reported to be, Madam Pendragon. This pleasures me immensely."

"It is not my intention to *pleasure* you, Mr. Maxwell," she noted coolly. Though he remained silent and unmoving, his gaze intensified as light sparked in their depths, making her wonder if his eyes were not as dark as they'd first appeared. "Nor is it my intention to suggest a threat in my words. The simple truth is that you cannot compete with Pendragon's Pleasure House. Your club will fail." She smiled, silky smooth. "I hope only for you to avoid the inevitable embarrassment and loss. You would be better off re-establishing your club elsewhere. Might I suggest Bath or Edinburgh?"

He lowered his chin with a long, slow exhale as he removed his spectacles and laid them atop his desk. When he looked at her again, he kept his chin lowered and lifted only his gaze. "Madam Pendragon. It seems clear that you would not have come here if you did not fear the exact thing you deny. But I would like to assure you that my business is not a threat to yours in any form."

Annoyance filled her at his unshakeable poise and subtle condescension. But before she could respond, he leaned forward to prop his elbows on his desk as he looked intently into her eyes. "You see, our businesses could not be more dissimilar."

Her temper flared. Did he believe himself so damned superior, then?

Callista shifted in her chair and leaned forward to mimic his posture, folding her hands on the gleaming surface of his desk. Though the position pushed her breasts against the edge of her bodice, exaggerating her cleavage and lengthening her neck, she was surprised to see that his gaze flickered not to her bosom but to her leather-encased fingers. The flame that had sparked in her core at the first sight of this man flared.

Steeling herself against it once again, she tilted her head to reply in a cool tone. "No matter how covert your services or how boring the décor of your establishment, the truth cannot be changed. Your business, Mr. Maxwell, is fucking. And so is mine."

She didn't exactly think she would shock him with her crude choice of words, but she certainly didn't expect the reaction she got.

It started with a slow, almost gentle widening of his lips—as though he'd just been offered a favored sweet and was imagining how he'd savor it—followed by a glitter of unnamed intention in his eyes. "You are quite right, madam. And also very wrong."

Chapter Two

Callista eased back into her chair and ran her hand along the waist of her corseted bodice, past the curve of her hip, before smoothing out the drape of her skirts over her crossed legs. Arching a brow, she gave a little sigh. "When it comes to the nature of my business, I am never wrong."

His sharp, glittering gaze never left hers despite the temptation she offered in her lounging figure. Even so...whatever he was thinking caused a spark of heat to flare brightly in his eyes.

Callista saw it. She *felt* it. Like a bolt of white fire angling straight through her center, she felt it.

Still holding her gaze, he straightened in his seat and put his spectacles back on.

Callista honestly couldn't decide if he was more unsettling with them or without. The man was indescribably handsome. Virile. Unexpected.

"I would never question your expertise, madam. However, I do believe it is time to address the true purpose of your visit."

"And what do you perceive the true nature of my visit to be?" she asked disdainfully.

He lowered his chin. "You are a clearly a woman of discernment. One who appreciates knowledge and discretion in equal measure. You have come to me for answers. And as I said earlier...I shall endeavor to satisfy you." The corner of his mouth lifted. "But first, would you like a drink?"

Anticipation sparked inside Callista. It was an interesting tack he'd taken. But she possessed an agile mind and unwavering resolve. "Brandy," she answered with an easy smile.

He opened a drawer in his desk and withdrew from it a bottle of fine French brandy and two snifters. After pouring two fingers into each glass, he rose to his feet and started around the wide desk. As he neared her position in the chair, she finally saw that his eyes were a very pale gray. Nearly silver. Despite his controlled manner, there was a predator's gleam in their depths.

Reaching her side, he extended one of the snifters. "If you would indulge me, madam, it would be my pleasure to explain."

A thrill went through her at his low-spoken words, but she hesitated. Stupidly. This was exactly why she'd come here. To get a sense of what he offered that had inspired such loyalty in his patrons. To learn the secret to how he'd formed a base of understated power and undeniable success in such a short time. She *needed* to know what she was up against.

Yet, as she looked up at his towering form—taller and broader than she'd realized—and noted the way he cradled the glass of brandy in his large palm, she got the oddest sense he was offering something she wasn't ready to accept.

Just take the blasted drink before he thinks you're daft. Or worse—afraid.

Affecting a tone of boredom, she accepted the brandy. "Do not expect me to be impressed, Mr. Maxwell."

He nodded in acknowledgement as he lifted his glass to swirl it in the firelight. "I am aware of your great accomplishments, Madam Pendragon. A gentleman cannot step foot in London without hearing tales of a woman of insurmountable grace and influence. A woman capable of bringing the most powerful men in Britain to their knees—and having them beg for more." Silver eyes caught hers in a quick snare. "A woman of indescribable beauty and fierce ambition. To achieve such success, one would have to possess extensive experience and infinite intuition. I've no doubt you can claim both in abundance. But I might just surprise you."

Callista hid the distrust his words aroused with a graceful shrug. No man offered such pretty compliments without expecting something in return. Yet somehow, when he spoke in such a way, it felt more like a restating of fact than flattery. She had to admit...Erik Maxwell possessed a great deal of charm within his restrained manner.

Crossing in front of her, he took a seat in the chair beside her.

Watching at him from beneath the sweep of her lashes, she couldn't help noting his patrician profile and athletic manner of movement—economical, relaxed yet dignified. He was a man who knew himself and trusted what his body was capable of. No doubt, he committed to a regular exercise regimen to maintain a superior degree of strength, endurance, and vitality.

That or he frequently enjoyed other, more pleasurable ways to promote a healthy physique.

To keep herself from wondering exactly how physically energetic a lover Erik Maxwell might be, she shifted in her seat, leaning toward him. The new position created deep, sensuous curves in her figure as she lifted her brandy. "By all means, Mr. Maxwell, surprise me."

He removed his spectacles again, this time resting them atop his thigh—his solid, hard-muscled thigh. He looked a little older without the glass shielding the darker shadows of experience in his eyes. She was also able to detect the gleam of self-awareness in their depths and spied the fine lines fanning out from the corners. The evidence of age in his features supported his calm air of casual arrogance while avoiding any suggestion of world-weariness often seen in older men.

"Your devotion to discretion and the security of your patrons' personal business is well-known. It is for this reason alone that I am willing to tell you the truth, yet before we go further in this discussion, I must have your assurance that you will not speak of what I tell you to anyone else."

"Is it so scandalous?" she asked dismissively.

He tilted his head, and though amusement hovered around his mouth, his answer was given in all seriousness. "Some might consider it an unforgivable transgression. Either way, it involves a delicate and personal issue my clients wish to keep private. The true nature of what happens within the walls of Maxwell's cannot become common knowledge."

She was intrigued despite herself. "You have my assurance."

"Although you were correct in saying my business is *fucking*"—his lips formed the word in a way that made her low body tighten—"my club is not a brothel."

Callista arched her brows. "Of course it is, Mr. Maxwell. You provide sexual services for a fee. There is no way around it and no shame in admitting it."

Silver eyes found hers. "It is not my intention to cast shame on the profession, madam. When managed well and safely, brothels offer valuable amenities to our societies by providing a welcome space for people to explore their desires and proclivities without fear of censure or risk to their person."

Callista was only slightly impressed. "Then why deny the association?"

"I do not deny it. In fact, I encourage it as it distracts from the truth. But Maxwell's does not deal in the business of pleasure for pleasure's sake." He lowered his chin. "Men do not come to me seeking such indulgences. They come to me for desperately needed guidance and instruction."

It was not what she'd expected. "Instruction?"

"Essentially, among other related services, I tutor gentlemen in how to seduce and make love to their wives."

Disbelief rolled through her at his words and her eyes widened as she stared back at him. She couldn't possibly have heard him right. "Surely, you jest."

"Not even a little."

"Mr. Maxwell, I have been involved in this trade for many years, most of which have been spent exclusively catering to men of high society. Men of that breed in particular are notorious for seeking their pleasure outside of the marriage bed for a very clear reason. Their wives are purchased through dowries and business arrangements to provide proper, well-pedigreed wombs for breeding. The ladies serve a strict and limited purpose. Mistresses and bawdy houses serve another." Callista shook her head with firm conviction. "No gentleman wishes to seduce his wife."

Dark brows lifted as he gestured with his brandy snifter. "My success suggests otherwise. There are, indeed, gentlemen who wish to enjoy the full gamut of pleasures—domestic, intimate, and sexual—with the woman they've taken as life mate."

"Then why bother with seduction? A husband's rights dictate that his wife must submit to his lustful needs." Skepticism made her voice harsh. "She has no choice in the matter."

"That is exactly the issue Maxwell's rectifies." The expression of the man beside her was earnest and thoughtful as he continued, "So many of these men grew to manhood with obscene amounts of wealth and prestige. They've easily obtained everything they wanted in their lives. Mistresses were not earned or won; they were beckoned with a ringed pinky finger. Lovers and friends flocked and fawned by the dozen. These men have always known well how to be pleasured, but only a rare few know how to go about pleasuring another with true emotion and generosity. And then there is the ridiculous notion that has pervaded humanity for too long—that a wife does not need or desire the same sort of attention in the bedroom that a mistress demands."

Callista waved a hand in dismissal. "The number of men who do not know how to properly pleasure their bed partner is not under debate. What I will never believe is that a man would go through the trouble of directing such efforts toward his wife."

"When a man's heart is involved, he will go to great lengths to achieve his goals."

Sitting back in her chair, Callista smirked. "Now I know it's a con. Men don't have hearts."

He did not immediately refute her bold claim but sat looking at her with a steady focus. Then he lifted his glass for a long sip. "Again, madam, I must disagree. Though many men may disregard the value of a loving, *satisfied* wife...some do not." He smiled. "I offer my services to those rare gentlemen."

"For an exorbitant fee."

"For a fair and reasonable fee when marital bliss is the reward."

"Bliss," she scoffed. "And what of these wives? What if they have no desire to deepen their relationships with their husbands?"

The light in his eyes darkened for a moment. "Coercion and manipulation are the antithesis of what I impart. Seduction is about *connection*. It is about knowledge and consideration and shared passion."

Meeting his intent gaze, she gave a slow shake of her head. "You speak of things that simply cannot be taught."

"Tell that to the countless men who have been enjoying more fulfilling marriages by becoming more generous, loving, sexually satisfying mates."

She laughed. "You can claim that all you'd like. But you cannot prove it."

He smiled. Slowly. Sensually. Intently. And that predator's gleam entered his gaze once again. "There is a way to prove the validity of my methods."

"I do not have time to observe your lessons, Mr. Maxwell. I have a business of my own to run."

"You misunderstand, madam. I'd like to demonstrate my methods. Allow me to seduce you."

As a thrill of delicate flames licked along the nerves of her body, Callista eyed him carefully and offered a short, indelicate laugh. "I am not susceptible to seduction, Mr. Maxwell, no matter how well practiced the techniques. I've seen behind the veil. It's where I spend all my time."

"I've promised to surprise you, madam." His voice was warm and textured. Though he didn't smile, Callista detected something anticipatory in his eyes. "Give me the chance."

"I won't go to bed with you."

But then he did smile. A quiet curve of firm, sensual lips. "No. Not tonight anyway." He replaced his spectacles and rose to his feet and stepped in front of her before offering his hand. "There is no need to rush."

For the first time since stepping into her rival's lair, she felt a frisson of alarm. She tilted her head to give him an assessing look, sliding her gaze up his trim form to his face, which was once again in shadow. Unable to read his expression, she lowered her attention to his hand. He possessed a wide palm and elegant fingers.

A shiver coursed through her. He thought to seduce her. And though the attempt would prove a failure despite her intense attraction to the man, she was admittedly very curious to see how he'd go about such a task. She wanted information about Maxwell's. It seemed he was willing to give it her. That it was in the form of a futile demonstration shouldn't matter.

After setting her brandy on the table beside her, she ignored his hand as she stood and smoothed her hands down the bodice of her black gown. "I shall give you until the end of the year."

"That's in twelve days."

Callista shrugged and moved to step past him. "If you doubt your methods…"

"I've no doubts." The weight of promise in his voice brought her to a stop. Their gazes met at an intimate distance.

"You're rather sure of yourself." The husky tone of her voice could not be fully disguised.

"With good reason."

Callista narrowed her gaze to disguise the effect his words had on her. "If you fail to prove anything beyond your own hubris, you will close your doors and leave London."

It was bold move.

"Agreed," he replied easily. "Are you available tomorrow evening?"

"Evenings are difficult for me," she replied as she slipped past him with a swish of her black skirts and started across the room to the door. It was time for her to leave before she started to regret coming in the first place. Or he thought to demand something in return if he should happen to succeed. Not that it would have mattered what boon he demanded since she had no doubt he would fail quite fantastically.

"I'll arrange something," he replied, undaunted by her evasion.

Callista lifted her hand in a wave over her shoulder. "You do that, Mr. Maxwell. I'll see myself out."

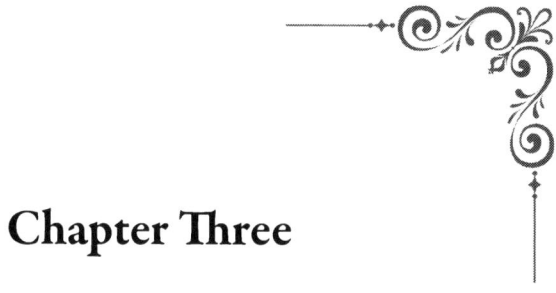

Chapter Three

Erik was still as he watched the dynamic woman walk away. The regal tilt of her head and purposeful stride contrasted in a fascinating way with the deeply sensual movement of her hips.

Once she stepped out of sight, he released a slow breath and leaned back against the edge of his desk.

His body was drawn taut. From head to toe, he felt primed and ready for action. The woman had worked him over with barely any effort. Though he was relatively certain she hadn't detected his fierce, consuming attraction, he was just as confident that if she ever did turn an eye toward him with the intention of seduction, he'd be in serious trouble.

When he'd first arrived in London, he'd learned a great deal about the woman behind the success of Pendragon's Pleasure House. It had only been a matter of time before he'd expected her to arrive at his club.

Madam Pendragon had proven to be the most captivating female Erik had ever encountered. With the ethereal beauty of a seraph and the commanding presence of a sorceress, Pendragon would undoubtedly prove to be a force unlike any he'd ever come up against.

Anticipation rushed through him.

He couldn't remember the last time he'd looked forward to something so intensely. His offer to seduce her had been impulsive but he had no desire to take it back, despite its many risks. One of the first things he told his clients was that they needed to be certain of their motivation and desired outcome. Seduction—as he taught it—was a serious endeavor. The effects of which had the potential to affect not only the seduced but also inevitably the seducer.

It had been a long time since he'd taken a lover. Once he'd begun to help men in realizing the full scope of pleasure and enjoyment to be found in their marriages, he'd found casual affairs unsatisfying.

But he'd never encountered a woman he wanted so intensely upon one brief meeting as he did Madam Pendragon. Everything about her attracted him. Her regal confidence, her sensual form, the shrewd gleam in her gaze, and the subtle twist of disdain in her smile.

Erik paced around his desk to stare down into the fire. He imagined stripping away her calculating aloofness and brash arrogance just as he'd remove the many layers of her fine clothing. What might be revealed beneath the black brocade and bewitching authority? Would he find a hot and fiery core within her cold ambition? Or was she made of steel throughout?

Twelve days to convince the bold woman she belonged in his bed. He'd have to be careful. His mouth curved as a thrill of anticipation coursed through his blood. He was up to the challenge.

WHEN ERIK SENT THE invitation to Madam Pendragon's attention at her business address in the very early hours of the morning, he hadn't expected a prompt response and hadn't gotten one. The answer he eventually received just a few hours ago, however, gave him a breath of insight into the woman's nature.

His message had requested her company for a late lunch at a location of her choice. Erik graciously offered to come for her in his carriage at an hour best suited to her full schedule.

Her reply was brief. An address. A time. And the assurance that she could manage her own way to the restaurant.

It was another challenge. He'd have to be resourceful—which he always was—and he'd have to be exceedingly quick.

The most popular oyster bar in Covent Garden was not typically open for business at such an early hour, but the owner had agreed to make an exception for a healthy fee. Despite the very late notice, the restaurant was staffed to accommodate their two guests with the manager agreeing to take care of them personally.

Erik arrived early to ensure all was in readiness, then sat at a table with a view of the door and waited.

The woman arrived promptly at the appointed hour, entering the establishment with bold confidence. The restaurant's manager rushed forward to greet her at the door as Erik rose to his feet. Across the small restaurant, he watched as she released the fastenings of her black velvet pelisse to reveal the scarlet gown beneath. The manager draped her pelisse over his arm as he gestured toward their table. She murmured something to the man and he backed away. As she approached Erik, he noted how her stunning gown molded to her figure, accentuating the deep, luscious curves while the stiff bodice lovingly cupped and lifted her full breasts, creating a lush setting for three ropes of black pearls. She wore no hat or veil today and her fair hair was piled atop her head in loose curls. As she neared, he could see that the cold December air had brought pink to her cheeks and a glitter to her green eyes.

"Madam," he greeted with a bow of his head, "I am enchanted."

Red lips curved into a tempered smirk. "Of course you are."

He smiled at the jaded tone in her voice and thought he might have seen a responding twitch in her lips.

Once they were both seated at the small wooden table, the manager appeared at their table to ask if they'd like to start their meal with champagne or some other refreshment.

Pendragon replied first, offering a half smile as she noted her choice. "I'd like a stout, please."

"Of course, madam," the manager said before glancing to Erik in inquiry.

"The same."

"Right away, sir."

Neither spoke as they waited for the drinks, choosing instead to openly assess each other.

The previous day in his club, Erik had sensed this woman's intuitive nature. Her sparkling gaze had a way of making the observed feel vulnerable and exposed. It was no different today. Though it did not bother him at all to fall under her intent perusal, it was clear she could unsettle a man with no more than a fleeting glance if she chose.

He appreciated that.

He admired the severity and tenacity it took for a woman to gain the kind of wealth and power this one had in a world so dominated and desecrated by men. But he also knew such endless ambition and resolve often required a person to sacrifice—or at the very least, carefully conceal—their softer elements.

After their stouts were brought out and the manager retreated once again, Erik raised his glass in a toast. "To the next twelve days."

She lifted her glass in a graceful salute. "Eleven, Mr. Maxwell."

He smiled. "The day is not over yet."

"True," she acquiesced, "but I hardly think you'll have me splayed across this table before we finish lunch."

She accented the statement by brushing her hand across the table. She wore red gloves today. Satin, reaching up to her elbows. Erik immediately envisioned her wearing nothing but the gloves, her lush body draped in sultry abandon across the bare wood surface of their table as he stepped between her parting thighs.

The woman's gaze narrowed. A knowing smirk twisted her reddened lips. "I can see you are now imagining exactly that, though I struggle to believe you are the type of man to indulge in even a little bit of daytime debauchery."

He lowered his chin to reply in a tone of dark confession. "You know better than to judge a man by his outward presentation, madam."

She searched his gaze for a long moment before replying in a heavy murmur, "I do indeed."

Their conversation was briefly paused as a wide tray of chilled oysters was brought to the table.

As his dinner companion removed her gloves by tugging at each of her fingertips before sliding the satin free, Erik was surprised by what was revealed. A tattoo of a black winged dragon graced the pale skin of her inner arm. The serpent's tail encircled her wrist like a permanent bracelet while the creature stared out with green eyes as sharp and penetrating as the lady's own gaze.

He glanced up to see she had noticed his intent perusal. Rather than feign disinterest, he reached his hand across the table and tilted his head in question. "May I?"

A fine blonde eyebrow arched and he got the impression most people did not openly comment on the tattoo. Without a word, she extended her hand toward him.

Her hand fit perfectly in the cradle of his. Pressing his thumb to the soft center of her palm, he slowly drew her hand closer so he could study the intricate detailing in the creature's scales and wings and its noble expression of disdain. The artwork was stunning. Though it was a decidedly European depiction of the mythical beast, Erik hadn't seen a tattoo of such quality since his years in Asia. Unable to stop himself, he lifted his other hand to trace the design with his fingertip. From the dragon's angular head, along the curving coil of its powerful body, following the elegant lines of its tail around the delicate bones of the lady's wrist to the spiked, arrow-point tip.

A flawless depiction of grace, power, violence, and sensuality.

Though he perused the tattoo intently, he did not miss the subtle rise of gooseflesh on her skin in reaction to his light touch, nor did he miss the way her fingers curled involuntarily toward her palm when his fingertip reached the delicate skin of her wrist. When he shifted his hold to continue the soft caress along the individual lines of her palm, he was immeasurably pleased that she did not pull away.

"Why the dragon?" he asked as he lifted his gaze back to hers.

The green of her eyes had darkened during his exploration and her eyelids had grown slightly heavy, shielding the secrets of her thoughts. Heat swirled instantly through his blood in response. It amazed him how swiftly and intensely his lust was triggered by this woman.

"Dragons guard their treasures fiercely and indiscriminately," she replied. "Any fool who'd covet the dragon's possessions can expect a fiery death."

Erik gave a short nod. "You chose the symbol as a warning."

Her hand tensed briefly in his. "That's correct."

"How many men have you been forced to light aflame?"

Her lips twitched as she gave a graceful shrug of her bare shoulders. The gesture was both dismissive and suggestive at the same time. "I've lost count."

He had no doubt of that. "Fools," he murmured thickly.

"Every single one," she agreed in voice of subtle steel. Her green eyes stared intently into his for a long, silent moment before she withdrew her hand from his. He knew better than to try to hold her.

The oysters were the best he'd enjoyed since arriving in England while the stout proved to be a perfect pairing. They ordered a second round as the remnants of their meal was cleared from the table.

Erik relaxed in his chair as his body embraced the languid aftermath of a good meal. In contrast, his mind remained fiercely alert and focused on the enigmatic woman across from him. He'd known from the onset that seducing the celebrated madam would not be easy. He didn't want easy.

He wanted her. Plain and simple. From the moment he'd watched her approach him in his office the previous day. The undeniable strength of purpose she possessed and the dynamic, sensual, almost ruthless confidence she embodied made his blood simmer and his cock stand. But more than the lust she inspired, it was the way she ignited his mind that attracted him most intensely.

In her presence, he had to be vigilant and shrewd. He could not rest on a superior intellect to retain an upper hand as he so often did. He enjoyed the way she challenged him with her jaded disbelief and brash arrogance. She was formidable. No doubt.

But he was no fumbling lad.

"Have you always lived in London?" he asked.

With a knowing smile, she eased back in her chair. "Have we reached the point in our meal where we disclose our heartbreaking backstories?"

"I want nothing you aren't willing to give."

She arched a brow at that but didn't refute him. "My story is no different than many others. Born and raised in the rookery until my morally destitute drunk of a father tried to sell me for a bottle of gin. I preferred to make my own way, instead. As many girls do, I quickly went from the gin shop to the bawdy house. It wasn't long before I decided how much control I was willing to allow a pimp, which turned out to be not a damn bit." Erik smiled at that and she smiled back. "I fought hard to get free and claim the right to protect myself and run my business by my own rules."

"Not an easy feat."

"Nothing worth keeping comes easily," she noted coolly.

Though he would have agreed with her, he made no reply.

"And you?" she asked with a tilted smirk. "What is your story?"

Erik leaned forward to rest his elbows on the table. "I was born into an acting troupe that traveled all across Europe and parts of Asia. Such a childhood instilled a wanderlust in my soul that continued throughout my life. I was not very old when I started attracting amorous attention. Once I realized the benefits to be found in certain arrangements with my admirers, I left the troupe and fashioned myself as a bit of a Lothario."

He looked down at his hands. "Those years of hedonism provided material wealth beyond any I ever had before. It also gave me a range and depth of experience that proved far more valuable." Lifting his gaze without raising his chin, he met the shielded gaze of the woman across from him as a smile tugged at his mouth. "It turns out that when gentlemen of fine pedigree and sophistication direct their passion and creativity toward their mistresses, it leaves their wives...rather hungry."

Pendragon's brows lifted. "I'm sure you were quite happy to satiate those poor ladies."

"Neglect of a woman's desires is one of the greatest wastes of human existence. I provided pleasure and an opportunity for these women to release inhibition and explore what satisfied them. It was a worthy practice until I began to notice what was missing in the interactions between myself and my paramours."

"What was that?" Though the woman was practiced in feigning a subtle disinterest, Erik detected the light of curiosity in her gaze.

"Intimacy," he replied simple. "True intimacy that can only be developed over time with someone you trust. A partner in life as well as in the bedroom. The kind of intimacy that grows between two people who are committed to each other. In hearing of how unhappy my lovers were in their marriages, I began to understand how the pleasure found in truly passionate, deeply intimate lovemaking is essential to such unions."

"Such a noble perspective." Her lovely features tightened with a smile of superiority. "But unrealistic. Men will always seek out new flesh to plunder."

"Not men who truly love their wives."

"Love," she scoffed. "No matter how enamored they might be on their wedding day, men *always* grow bored with their pious, perfect mates. If they didn't, I wouldn't have a business."

Erik nodded. "It is true. For some. But I am not talking of those men. My focus is on the gentlemen who have a true desire to cultivate such a relationship with the woman they have taken as life mate."

Giving up her relaxed posture, the madam leaned forward to rest her elbows on the table in a posture that matched his own. Her green eyes flashed. "Tell me, Mr. Maxwell, are you also married?"

He paused, understanding the antagonizing note in her voice. Meeting her green gaze with steady focus, he replied, "No, madam. I am not nor have I ever been."

"Then what exactly can you offer these men?"

Erik smiled, appreciating her skepticism and her demand for explanation. She was not one to simply accept what anyone told her. She'd need to experience something personally before agreeing it was possible. This was likely the only reason she'd agreed to allow him to demonstrate his practice.

He lowered his voice. "We've previously established that far too many men do not know how to properly make love to a woman. I share the knowledge and techniques I developed in my time as lover to many varied women. But more important than that...I assist them in understanding how to cross that important bridge from gentleman husband to thoughtful, passionate life partner. It often requires a complete overhaul of their trained way of thinking and a destruction of the false assumptions that perpetrated about the fair sex. These men come to me because they want to become a lover and partner to their mates. I help them to see their wife as a woman first with all of the needs—base and exalted—a woman possesses. The seduction and pleasuring come rather easily after that."

Pendragon's gaze was narrow and assessing as she looked back at him. The tension in her jaw was barely discernable, but he saw it. She almost appeared...angry. Interesting.

"You are obviously very pleased with yourself," she noted.

"I have witnessed great love stories unfold before my eyes. It is an honor to be a part of it."

"That is a load of bullshit."

Erik laughed. Her blunt way of talking caught him off guard on occasion. He enjoyed it. "I can understand why you'd think so. But I assure you, I mean every word."

The woman eyed him over the rim of her glass as she took a sip before saying with disparagement in her tone, "You are a sentimentalist."

Was he? Probably.

He shrugged. "I'm also logical, analytical, and sometimes a bit overly focused. Ultimately, I trust in what my experiences have revealed to me."

"And what is that?"

"People need love." When she rolled her eyes, he smiled. "Don't get me wrong, madam. The pleasures of the flesh are also absolutely necessary, but when sexual satisfaction combines with true emotion within a devoted partnership, something wonderful is created."

"A delusion?"

Erik caught her gaze and held it. "I promise you. It is very real."

The lady set her unfinished stout on the table and stood. Erik rose as well, allowing himself a quick perusal of her stunning figure.

"While I appreciate your candid explanation, Mr. Maxwell," she began as she slid her gloves on, smoothing the satin from her fingertips to her elbows, "it reveals a significant flaw in your planned demonstration."

He lifted a brow. "Does it?"

Her red lips widened in a smile that was more genuine than most he'd received from her. "We are not married. And I am not a high-society gentlewoman."

Erik watched with deep appreciation as she turned and sauntered to the door where the manager was waiting with her fur-lined coat. She stepped out into a light swirl of winter snow.

Chapter Four

The next morning, a small package arrived at Pendragon's. The card addressed it to Madam Pendragon and also included an invitation to the theater for the following evening. It was signed simply, *E.M.*

Callista took the wrapped box up to her private suite to open. Inside she found a stunning pair of red elbow-length gloves made of a leather so fine and supple it felt like butter against her skin when she slid her fingers into place and smoothed the gloves up her arms.

Recalling the look in Maxwell's eyes when she'd done the same before leaving the oyster bar the day before, her core tightened with an intense jolt of desire.

The man had proven to be unexpected. For the most part, he possessed an air of thoughtful patience and self-assured restraint. She'd already ascertained that not much flustered the man. He was not one to waver under criticism nor did he appear particularly vulnerable to female manipulation. His demeanor was almost studious in nature.

Yet…he'd shown her more than once that a wickedness resided beneath his stoic façade. There was heat in his eyes when he looked at her. And a gleam that suggested the sort of knowledge that came only from extensive experience.

It made her want to indulge in a little of that experience herself.

She wouldn't, of course. And not just because he declared his intention to seduce her as a means of demonstrating his methods. If she wanted a man, she didn't need him to seduce her. She simply welcomed him to her bed. It had always been that way.

And wasn't that exactly why she'd been without a lover in far too long?

The act had grown stale and uninteresting. The truth was, even though she operated the most infamous and exclusive brothel in London, she rarely thought of sex in a personal context. Her last bed partner had been a few years ago now and she hadn't felt like she'd been missing anything. There was nothing new to explore. One man was much like another.

Erik Maxwell was surely no different.

Her unexpected sexual awareness of the man might simply have been triggered by the fact that she couldn't fully read him. She knew men. She knew them well. Knowing what men needed before they knew themselves had been the focus of her life for more than two decades. Maxwell was the first in a long time whose motivations and desires still remained unclear to her after two encounters.

The anomaly was the only reason she so readily accepted his invitation. Besides, it wouldn't exactly be fair to declare his efforts at seduction futile if she never allowed him opportunities to employ his supposed skills.

Typically, she'd never leave her place on an evening they were open for business. However, with the Christmas holiday arriving in only a few days, business had slowed tremendously as gentlemen spent more time than usual with family and at intimate parties. It was exactly why one of her biggest events of the year occurred between Boxing Day and the New Year. Free of familial obligations, her clientele always proved ready for more risqué revelry.

The reply she sent to Maxwell's invitation indicated that she would meet him at the theater. She dressed in a gown of black silk beneath an overlay of red lace netting embroidered with a snaking pattern around the hem and over her bodice. Accessorized with her favorite strand of black pearls, her new red leather gloves, and a black velvet cloak, she was finally satisfied with the drama in her appearance.

The signature colors and eye-catching, seductive style was a crucial aspect of the infamy that surrounded her. Madam Pendragon was a character who'd developed out of a need for Callista to stand out at a time when she'd been just another pretty prostitute. Her ambitions had always reached far beyond whatever current status she found herself in, but at one point, she came to the realization that men wanted more than a pretty face and a good fuck. They craved fantasy and the kind of drama they could enjoy and then walk away from.

Madam Pendragon provided that and so much more.

Callista's dedication to the persona had grown until she'd lost sight of any delineation between herself and the madam. They had long ago become one and the same. Not even her brother—the only person who'd known her as she'd been before all the production she surrounded herself with—saw much of Callista anymore.

It was fine.

Callista Hale had been a rookery brat, raised in poverty and violence. She'd scrounged and clawed and bit to escape the muck and soot of her origins. Though that angry, desperate girl would always be a part of her, there was no reason for anyone to ever become acquainted with her.

The theater in Covent Garden was teeming with people dressed in their finest.

Callista swept past them all, not bothering to glance toward any of the shocked or curious faces of people who wondered how she could have the audacity to show her face amongst such noble citizens. Pshaw! Those who knew better—the gentlemen who frequented her wicked establishment—kept their stern faces carefully averted, trying desperately to avoid her notice lest she indicate by word or deed their association with her in front of their precious wives.

Idiots!

Each and every one of them knew her policies on discretion and privacy. She made sure they followed her rules strictly or they risked being banned from her place or worse. Only in their self-guilt would they think she'd even consider revealing their dirty little secrets.

Idiots. Every one of them.

"Madam."

Her inner tirade was brought to an abrupt halt as Mr. Maxwell stepped in front of her, seemingly out of nowhere.

She was rarely caught off guard and his sudden appearance caused her to stiffen before she recalled the grand audience around them. With a slow, sensual smile, she continued forward to offer her hand to her escort for the evening.

"Mr. Maxwell. A pleasure, I'm sure." He took her offered fingers and bowed his head over them. When he straightened, a subtle smile turned up the corner of his mouth and his pale gray eyes stared intently into hers. He wouldn't have missed the fact that she was wearing his gift, yet he chose not to comment on it.

"You are exceptionally lovely this evening."

Callista accepted the compliment with a tilt of her head before she slid her attention down the length of his masculine form. She'd thought him handsome before, but in his black evening wear and stark white cravat, he looked far more distinguished and more delectable than any of the lords surrounding them. "No spectacles?"

If he was put off by her comment, he didn't show it as he gave a half shrug. "I prefer opera glasses when at the theater." Gesturing to the side, he asked, "The show will start shortly. Shall we take our seats?"

When people attended the theater, it was to observe the other attendees as much as it was to watch the performers on stage, which meant the seats were rarely occupied by the start of the show as people continued to mingle in the lobby well into the evening.

It seemed Mr. Maxwell did not intend to follow that trend.

"If you wish," she replied lightly, then had to hold her breath as he smoothly stepped to her side. After tucking her hand into the bend of his elbow, he maintained a respectable distance as he led her through the crowded room. His proper decorum was disconcerting. It had been a long time since she'd been with a man who played the role of escort. If she went anywhere with a member of the opposite sex, she was leading the way.

His stride remained unhurried as he brought her first to the cloak room to check her outer garment before passing right by the refreshment counter to take her up the stairs to the upper seating level. When he stopped outside the drawn curtains of a private box, Callista glanced at him curiously.

He smiled at her questioning look and swept the curtain aside to allow her to pass onto the darkened balcony. "After you."

"How extravagant," she noted.

"I've a few friends in high places."

Though the box held seats for up to six people, it appeared it had been reserved for just the two of them. A table had been set up with chilled champagne along with a bottle of brandy.

As Maxwell stepped up behind her, the curtain leading to the hall fell closed. Standing back from the balcony railing as she was, she couldn't see the floor seating at all and the stage curtains were still closed. All she could hear were the sounds of the orchestra playing softly and subtle movement of her skirts as she turned to face the man behind her.

"I think I like your friends," she whispered.

His answering laugh was rich and warm. A man's laugh shouldn't be so physically affecting. Shaking off her reaction, she stepped forward to take one of the seats.

"A drink, madam?"

"Champagne." She was in the mood for something light and sparkly to balance the velvet darkness surrounding them. Just because she'd decided to allow him the opportunity to seduce her didn't mean she intended to make it easy for him.

After handing her a crystal flute and taking one for himself, he took the seat beside her.

"Thank you for joining me this evening."

Callista glanced aside at him. Keeping her expression neutral, she noted the way his black and silver hair swept back from his broad forehead in soft waves. Without his glasses, the predatorial gleam of his gaze was poignant and sharp beneath thick brows, even in the darkened theater. But his mouth was relaxed and soft. The upper lip was modestly arched while the lower was full and lush. It was a deliciously kissable mouth.

He waited patiently for her to finish her perusal, without fidgeting or glancing away. He was comfortable being under direct observation, which usually indicated a person who was confident they had nothing to hide or someone who was so accustomed to deception they had no fear of detection.

Which was he?

"I imagine your business takes a great deal of your time," he added.

"It does," she finally replied as she sipped her drink. Though in truth, the demand on her time was far less than it had been even five years ago. Pendragon's Pleasure House was well staffed and had reached a point when it could essentially run itself.

"Is it difficult for you to get away?" He gestured toward the stage. "For diversions such as this, I mean."

She arched a brow. "Not particularly. I simply prefer to spend my time doing what I enjoy. I enjoy business, Mr. Maxwell. I enjoy success and profit and the wealth and influence that have come with it."

He smiled then. Lowering his chin, he asked earnestly, "And what about life outside of Pendragon's?"

Callista scoffed. "There is no life outside of Pendragon's. It is me and I am it." She looked away from him to casually scan the slowly filling theater below. Already she spotted several of her clients, some of them escorting their wives, others ensconced in the shadows with their mistress. Without turning her head back to the man beside her, she asked, "Why all the questions? What will you do with my secrets once you've dug them all up?"

"Nothing." His voice was velvety and dark. The accent she'd become accustomed to thickened with his whisper. "Secrets are for keeping, madam."

She slid him a glance from the corners of her kohl-rimmed eyes. "Well, I have none. Anyone who wants to know about me will have little trouble gathering the facts of my life. There have been many who have sought to discredit me over the years. Rivals who have tried to sink my ambitious rise. They have all failed. I hide nothing, so there is nothing to discover."

He shook his head. "That is blatantly untrue."

Callista narrowed her gaze.

Leaning forward, he noted smoothly, "What of the secrets in your soul? The private longings of your heart?"

Her laugh was harsh and cold. "My heart? That offensive thing? Discarded long ago. And if I've a soul, it's far too blackened to possess any tender morsels for you to feast upon."

The sound he made was a low hum and his eyes sparked with silent intention as he leaned back again and raised his glass for a long sip of champagne.

She could see he didn't believe her—that he fully expected to uncover some long-buried yearning she'd yet to fulfill. Then he'd likely press upon that weakness, mold it and reshape it to suit his purpose, until she believed he was the only one capable of filling whatever void he believed to be inside her.

The amount of arrogance men managed to cultivate had long ago ceased to astound her. Yet she found herself disappointed to witness it yet again in this man. Had she actually been hoping he might be different? Smarter. More experienced. Less self-obsessed. Truly interested.

As the lights lowered around them and the curtains drew open upon the stage, Callista shifted her full attention to the scene unfolding before her, intentionally and completely ignoring the man beside her.

The performance was a well-known Italian opera she'd seen many times before. It was a farcical comedy about bedroom escapades and secret lovers and she'd always enjoyed the way it depicted sexual congress as a lighthearted, pleasurable diversion. She never could abide the operas about vestal virgins and perceived betrayals that invariably ended in someone's untimely death.

She actually loved the opera. It provided one of the rare instances in her life that allowed for true escapism. To her surprise and appreciation, Maxwell was content to allow her to enjoy the performance without overwhelming her with unwanted small talk or attempts at flirtation or other such annoying interruptions. Most men, if they got an object of their desire to join them in a private theater box enshrouded in darkness, would have made definite attempts at furthering their agenda. But Maxwell hadn't attempted any sly caresses. Nor had he leaned close to whisper in her ear at any point during the performance.

As the curtains fell on the final scene and the lights came up, Callista rose to her feet to applaud the show. The man beside her stood as well. His shoulder briefly brushed hers, but when she turned to look up at him, his face was in profile as he directed his focus to the stage, where the performers were taking their bows.

After a moment, he turned to meet her gaze. His expression was unreadable, but something in his eyes unsettled her.

"Shall we make our way down?" he asked. "Or would you prefer to wait until the crowd has dispersed?"

"There's no need to wait."

There was just a brief pause, then he gave a nod as he gestured for her to precede him from the box. Once past the heavy curtain, he offered his arm once again. She accepted his escort despite the odd tension that had settled in her being. Most frustratingly, she couldn't quite pinpoint the source of her discomfort.

Becoming lost in her thoughts, as she often did after a particularly transporting performance, it took a bit to sense the subtle shift in the energy of the man beside her. Glancing up at him, she could not detect anything overt in his manner. Still, she sensed an increased alertness in his being. A sharper focus in his gaze as he looked out over the flow of theatergoers making their way from their seats.

When they entered the more open common area, she finally had to ask, "What has you so intent, Mr. Maxwell?"

The look he gave her was one of question mingled with a slight suggestion of concern. "Do they always stare in such a way?"

She cast a dismissive glance about the crowd then shrugged. "I suppose. I don't typically bother myself with the rude habits of strangers."

He chuckled. "Have you any idea how many men and women are both covetous and intimidated by just the sight of you passing through their midst?"

Callista met his gaze with a sardonic lift of her brow. "Of course I do. As well they should be."

"Indeed," he agreed with a slow smile, "the lady dragon is fearsome and sensual beyond compare." Dipping his head closer to hers, he added, "I wonder if they see the superior intelligence and unique beauty of the woman within the awe-inspiring creature?"

Arching her brows, Callista replied, "Woman and beast are one and the same."

He tilted his head and studied her quietly for a moment. "Are they? I am not so sure."

They reached the cloak room, and when the attendant retrieved Callista's heavy black garment, Maxwell took it before she could. Shaking it out, he held it up with a subtle light of challenge in his eyes.

Inexplicably, she hesitated. But only for a moment. There was no reason to resist such a gesture. She'd had men touch her in ways that went far beyond this simple act. So why did it feel so damned unsettling when she turned in place, giving him her back?

The sound of her cloak brushing the skirts of her gown told her he was stepping closer, though it would have been obvious anyway by the warmth of his body at her back and the scent of sandalwood drifting through her senses.

The weight of the velvet touched her bare shoulders first, then the gentle press of his hands smoothing the material in place. His touch was confident without being intrusive. The act was not overtly sexual in any way. In fact, it was quite platonic. Yet, for a second, she stopped breathing, wondering if he would use the opportunity to extend his caress, perhaps by sliding his hands down her arms. Or drifting a fingertip across her nape or along the outer edge of her ear. Or he could step closer—press his hard, trim body to hers.

She knew for a fact she'd fit perfectly against him like this. Her back to his chest, her buttocks lush to his groin, her head tipped back against his shoulder so his mouth could access her throat. Perfect.

When he did nothing more than adjust the fall of her hood, she glanced over her shoulder at him, not even caring if her irritation showed in her face.

His smile was slow and knowing, which caused her irritation to deepen.

So, that had been his intention. To make her physically aware of his nearness, his touch, then leave her body wanting more. It was a common ploy. She shouldn't have fallen or it.

As he turned to retrieve his greatcoat, she took a moment to re-establish her natural grounding. To brush away any hint of sensual longing he might have inspired with his practiced torment.

"May I escort you to your carriage?" he asked, offering his arm once again.

Callista sighed. "If you must, though you should know the show of gallantry is utterly lost on me."

When her words inspired a gentle chuckle from the man, she realized with a jolt of shock that she'd made the jaded comment specifically for that purpose. Already, she'd come to understand that he enjoyed her cynical and blunt sarcasm. And she enjoyed his rare show of amusement far too much.

Rather than wait for the carriage to come around, by silent agreement, they started walking to where the carriage was parked a couple blocks down from the theater. The silence continued during the stroll along the dark, frozen pavement. A few light, drifting snowflakes swirled about in the winter air and Callista tipped her face to watch them dance against the backdrop that was Covent Garden.

Callista loved this part of London. She loved its grittiness and danger and how it existed at the very edge of the sophisticated societies who came to the neighborhood of excitement and risk. She loved how it blurred the lines between light and dark, sin and virtue, entertainment and survival.

There was a specific sort of energy here. Filled with ambition and a soul-deep hunger. That energy had fed her for years, until she'd gained a fat enough purse to buy her own place closer to the neighborhoods of the elite patrons she'd intended to service.

"Is it possible I'm witnessing an expression of contentment?" His tone was warm and carried only a hint of the seductive undertones he'd employed earlier in the evening.

Callista allowed a smile but didn't turn to look at him. In her current mood, she decided to be a bit magnanimous. "I suppose anything is possible."

"I know better than to assume my company is the cause. Will you share the thoughts inspiring such enjoyment?"

Having reached her carriage, Callista stopped and turned to face him. A few snowflakes sparkled in his hair and dusted the shoulders of his greatcoat. His mouth was soft, his gaze curious. He appeared almost harmless in the winter moonlight.

But regardless of what he wanted her to believe or how she occasionally found herself feeling almost comfortable and relaxed in his presence, he was her rival and her adversary.

She smiled—a stiff curving of lips that had grown chilled in the night air. "Come now, Mr. Maxwell, we both know you've less interest in my thoughts than you do in my perceived heart."

His expression didn't change at first. He simply stood in the light falling snow, looking handsomely distinguished and utterly self-possessed as his focus moved slowly over the details of her face. She oddly got the sense he was a bit...disappointed.

Then his manner slowly changed. She felt his shifting intensity like a vibrational wave. Her breath held and her leather-gloved hands curled into fists beneath the fall of her cloak.

"Madam Pendragon, I apologize for not having made myself clear since our first meeting." His brows lowered, shadowing his gaze, while his firm lips shaped the next words with carnal intent. "I am interested in *all* of you. Not only the softness of your skin or the lush heat between your thighs. I want to learn the rhythm of your heartbeat. Share in your deepest dreams and darkest pleasures. Such desires are undeniable." He leaned toward her to add in a heavy whisper, "As is my wish to become intimately acquainted with your shrewd and beautiful mind."

Despite the riot of sensations his words and voice and silver eyes triggered throughout her body, Callista hardened her expression and tilted her head to a condescending angle. "You don't want much, do you?"

"Just you, madam."

The heavy words sunk through her winter wear into her skin as light snowflakes drifted around them in the golden light of the street's gas lamp.

"You didn't expect it to be easy, did you?"

"Nothing worth keeping comes easily," he said, repeating a phrase she'd used when talking of Pendragon's.

Her stomach twisted.

It was a grave miscalculation on his part. This whole seduction was a ploy to get her off his back. She could believe he wanted her in his bed. Not many men didn't. But he'd made a mistake in implying he had any intention of *keeping* her.

Without a word, she turned and stepped into her carriage unaided by Mr. Maxwell or the groom who stood waiting beside the open door. As soon the door closed and the vehicle started moving, she put the arrogant man directly from her mind.

Chapter Five

Erik stood by the window of the private sitting room on the third floor of his club. A morning snowfall had caused the roads of London to become a slushy mess. But tonight was Christmas Eve and not even poor weather or wretched road conditions would keep people from attending their many soirées and dinner parties. The steady stream of carriages passing back and forth on the street below certainly attested to that fact. It was an evening devoted to intimate gatherings of family and friends to acknowledge and celebrate the holiday.

Tomorrow would bring long church services and family luncheons. Tonight was for revelry.

Turning his back on the scene, he crossed the room to the fireplace, where he added a couple more logs to keep the winter chill at bay. Standing there, he watched as the flames danced higher and sent a wave of heat and light into the room. He was not used to such cold weather. Though he'd traveled a great deal in his life, he had rarely been so far to the north during the colder months.

Despite how he often felt it, it appeared he wasn't too old for new experiences after all.

As his association with Madam Pendragon had also proven.

The woman was getting to him with her jaded green eyes, armored manner, and quick, sardonic wit. Though she was obviously determined to keep him at a distance, he reveled in those moments when her guard came down. When her full lips smiled in genuine pleasure and her eyes lit from within. She was proving to be as difficult to seduce as she'd declared herself to be. Difficult but not impossible.

Because Erik had seen desire sparking in the depths of her gaze. He'd felt the barely perceptible trembling of her fingers when he took her hand in his. The attraction he experienced for the enigmatic woman was not one-sided, but she was no novice to lust and she had her reasons for resisting her desire for him.

She didn't trust him and Erik couldn't blame her. The life she'd lived was a hard one. To achieve the degree of success she had would have taken complete and total devotion. Not for the faint of heart.

A woman like her would not fall for a false seduction. But there had been nothing deceitful or contrived in Erik's pursuit. He wanted her in every way. More than he'd ever wanted a woman before. There had been no lie present when he'd declared his interest in all of her. He never would have offered to seduce her if he hadn't already known in his soul that something more was supposed to exist between them.

But he'd never convince her to give their undeniable attraction a chance to expand into something deeper and more fulfilling if she didn't believe such even existed.

The staccato knock of his butler sounded on the door.

Erik gave a call to enter but did not turn away from the fire.

"You have a visitor, sir."

Turning his head, Erik watched as the woman who had been occupying his every thought lately sauntered into the room. Days ago, he'd advised his butler that unless he was with a client, he would be available to her at any time of the day or night and that she should be shown to his private quarters immediately if she called.

Even so, her appearance tonight was unexpected.

As the butler bowed from the room, closing the door securely as he did so, Erik turned his back to the fire so he could watch her approach.

Damn, but the woman made an exceptional entrance. Dressed tonight in a black satin gown that bared her shoulders and lush cleavage while accenting every lovely curve of her body, she was the archetypal seductress. Sinuous and strong, deeply sensual and utterly self-controlled. Erik was so bewitched by the liquid movement of her hips it took him a moment to see that she carried a bottle of brandy in her hand.

Anticipation rushed through him as he lifted his attention to the woman's face.

Green eyes reflected the dance of the flames behind him and lush red lips curved enticingly. After the way their night at the theater had ended, he wasn't sure if she'd continue meeting with him.

He should have expected to be surprised by this woman. She had come to him.

"Madam," he said as she reached him before the fireplace. "This is unanticipated."

Fine brows arched. "It shouldn't be." She lifted the bottle of brandy. "You couldn't have thought I'd enjoy this rare and very expensive bottle of brandy all by myself."

"I had thought you might enjoy savoring it in your quieter hours."

She gave a graceful shrug of her bare shoulders. "Some things are for savoring. Others are for enjoying with full, unadulterated gusto."

"And this brandy falls into the second category?"

"It does tonight."

"I'll get the glasses."

Erik crossed to a sideboard to collect two snifters, and when he turned back to face his guest, it was to see that despite the comfortable sofa and chairs positioned nearby, she had chosen instead to recline on the thick ivory-colored rug spread before the stone-carved hearth. Leaning to the side, she propped herself on one hand as the skirts of her black gown fanned about her legs, reflecting the light from the fire.

When she turned to look over her shoulder at his approach, there was a challenge in her bright, clever gaze, but also a hint of something he hadn't previously detected in the woman. A quiet, subtle sadness that spoke directly to the loneliness within himself.

Lowering himself to his knees, Erik sat back on his heels as he set the two glasses on the stone hearth. In a silent gesture, he extended his hand for the bottle, which she promptly handed off to him. After opening and pouring, he set the bottle aside and offered a snifter to the lady, who immediately lifted it in a toast.

"To cold winter nights and fine liquor."

"And even finer company," he added.

Her smile was fleeting as she lifted the glass and nearly drained it in one swallow.

Erik followed suit, then topped them off with another pour before settling into a more comfortable position. Then he turned his openly assessing focus on his unexpected companion while she directed her gaze toward the fire. She had to sense his blatant perusal but it did not appear to discomfit her in the slightest, and he was glad of that since it was not his intention to distress her. He simply found himself too fully intrigued by her to try to conceal his curiosity.

Curiosity and *longing*.

He couldn't deny that part. It was inseparable from his increasing feelings for her.

No doubt, she was very accustomed to men staring so keenly, though he suddenly hated the thought of being just one among likely countless admirers.

With a tilt of her head that was both haughty and coy, she slid a glance in his direction. "I assume since I was shown up here so directly, my visit did not interrupt anything important you might have been tending to."

Erik chuckled. "Not unless you count the silent cursing of winter weather to be important."

She made a rough sound of disgust as she lifted her glass for a drink. "I abhor this time of year."

"That is a strong statement."

"But a true one. Everyone bustles about promoting this ridiculous façade of *good cheer* and a *generous spirit*, when any other time of year, they are selfishly devoted to personal pleasures and hedonism. It's all so bloody false. And wretchedly dull."

"I take that to mean you do not celebrate the Christmas holiday."

"Only as I must. Christmas is best enjoyed by children and the faithful. I am neither."

"But you *do* have plans for tomorrow?"

She sighed and turned back to the flames. "My brother is insisting I join him and his family for a holiday dinner. He's being rather stubborn about it actually. Very annoying."

"Dinner does not appeal to you?"

She finished the amber liquor in her glass before reaching for the bottle to replace it. "Dinner is fine. I'm simply dreading everything that goes with it. Family is not my forte."

"They're a bunch of arseholes?" he prompted in a dry tone.

Her laugh was short but rich and real. "Oh, my brother is definitely an arsehole. But a tolerable one most of the time. His life has undergone some drastic changes recently. Good changes, I suppose, but they've prompted this unprecedented attempt at creating some sort of holiday tradition."

"There is nothing inherently terrible about tradition. Not when you understand that tradition is what you make it."

She slid him a skeptical glance. "Is that so?"

Erik swirled his brandy as he thought back to the pleasures of his childhood. "My troupe was made up of people from all over the world. We all brought our own beliefs and faiths with us. We found a way to blend these things into new traditions we shared together. Growing up with such freedom and non-judgement showed me how people from differing backgrounds and experiences can come together if they simply prioritize compassion and mutual respect."

She studied him silently from beneath the heavy sweep of her lashes. Erik remained still under her perusal as he stared intently back at her. The intelligence and bright calculation he admired so genuinely were ever present in her green gaze but there was a softening there as well, though it could simply be attributed to the brandy.

The woman was intimidating, to be sure. Self-assured and independent in ways many women were not. Clever, passionate, distrustful, arrogant, and mysterious. It was a singular experience to attempt the seduction of a woman who refused to let you know where you stood. Though he sensed her attraction to him and was delighted she'd chosen to come to him tonight, he knew better than to assume either of those things meant anything in regard to whether or not he would be successful in his endeavor.

She was too cynical and far too unpredictable.

But he was becoming more and more determined to know her. Not Madam Pendragon, who ruled London's world of sexual delights and pleasures untold. Erik wished to know the girl who'd left home young to claim sovereignty over herself and her future. The young woman who'd dreamed of having it all and having it all under *her* dominion.

With a depth and intensity that surprised him, he wanted the woman seated before him to find him worthy of not only her intimate time but also her most secret thoughts and unspoken dreams for the future. He was not a man to do anything half-measure and he'd known almost from the very start that he wanted this woman for everything she was, including those elements she carefully kept hidden from the rest of the world.

As his thoughts continued to swirl through the unsettling emotions she inspired, a small knowing smile curved her lips. "You're all the same, you know."

Though he suspected he knew what she was referencing, he still asked, "We are?"

"Men. Always wanting what you can't have."

"Are you referring to my desire for you?" he asked in a low tone.

"Of course," she replied with an elegant gesture and a manipulatively coy smile. "I can feel your hunger like heat in the air between us."

"There is no reason to deny it. I made clear at our last meeting what I want."

"That's right. All of me," she said sardonically as she sipped her brandy.

Setting his snifter to the side, he leaned forward—bringing the heat of his desire with him—until he could see the pupils of her eyes widen a moment before her lashes swept lower to conceal her reaction.

"Madam," he murmured in a tone heavy with truth. "I am no longer a young man. There is more of my life spread out behind me than what I expect to encounter ahead of me. With that understanding comes a certainty about what I want to fill the time I have remaining. If you still believe my pursuit of you has anything at all to do with business, you'd be horribly mistaken."

CALLISTA FOCUSED ON breathing as the force of his words shot through her like white-hot lightning. For a moment, it felt like his declaration changed her intrinsically. Her cellular makeup felt altered by his words, which told her something unexpected—she *had* believed it was all a business ploy on his part, and now that she knew it wasn't, everything was different.

Still, many years of self-preservation urged her to reply with sharp finality. "As I said previously," she noted with a smoothly forced smile, "you cannot have me."

"Not yet," he murmured, repeating the words he'd spoken to her once before.

The man's patience was awe-inspiring and irritating beyond belief. Now that she had been forced to acknowledge the truth and depth of his desire, which went beyond basic lust to something far more terrifying, she also had to admire his determination to stay the course of seduction with slow and steady intent.

Despite her constant resistance.

Callista glanced to the snifter cradled in her palm. She was due for another pour but realized she'd likely had more than enough already. She couldn't exactly recall what had prompted her to share the man's gift with him. Likely, it had simply been the desire not to enjoy the pleasure alone. But now that the lovely liquor had softened and warmed her body in such a delightful way and was starting to melt her insides, as well, she feared remaining in Mr. Maxwell's presence any longer.

She was liable to starting rethinking this whole seduction thing and that would not be good for her.

And why was that again?

It didn't matter.

Setting her glass aside, she rose to her feet in a graceful, sinuous motion. Unfortunately, she miscalculated the degree of her inebriation and her head spun for a moment as the world tipped precariously on its axis.

Maxwell noticed her slight loss of balance before she could correct it. Though still in the process of rising to his feet, he immediately grasped her waist to steady her. The heat and strength of his hands on her body, soaking through the thin layers of satin and silk, triggered a rush of desire through her blood. It swirled and spun then settled heavily in her center.

Foolish desire. Reckless need. Desperate longing.

Still holding her secure in his hands, he continued to his full height until they stood facing each other with bare inches between them. Callista knew real fear in that moment. Fear unlike any she'd experienced before because it touched a part of her she'd believed to be nonexistent.

"Shall I let you go?"

His low-spoken words could be taken as a request for assurance that she'd regained her balance. Or they could be taken as something else entirely. Callista chose to respond to the less detrimental option. Obviously.

"I won't tumble to the floor, I assure you."

He smiled. A devastating expression of subtle amusement and undeniable appreciation. Nothing seemed to dissuade this man.

His fingers tensed briefly against the muscles of her low back as his thumbs pressed firmly to her belly. Sensation erupted throughout her body, touching on every secret little corner of her being. Then he withdrew his hands, chilling her body with an intense sense of loss.

She shook it off.

"Although it's been a lovely evening, Mr. Maxwell, I must be off."

"I'll escort you home."

"I've been making my own way in the world for a very long time. I'll manage."

"Just because you can doesn't mean you have to."

For some reason, his words struck a chord within her. It both scared her and irritated her.

He wanted to insinuate himself into her life? Fine.

"If you really want to accompany me somewhere, join me for my brother's little get-together tomorrow."

His expression revealed only a hint of the surprise she'd anticipated.

"Is that a genuine invitation?"

She gave a casual shrug. "Why the hell not. At least I'd have someone to converse with. I'll be round to pick you up."

Chapter Six

"Your brother lives here?" Erik asked as Pendragon's carriage pulled to a stop in front of a palatial mansion in the heart of Mayfair.

The lady seated beside him tossed him a smirking smile as a groom opened the carriage door. "He does."

Erik stepped from the vehicle then turned to offer her his hand. As typical, there was a very slight hesitation before she slid her leather-clad fingers along his palm and allowed him to assist her to the pavement. "He is an aristocrat?"

Her laugh was a delicate snort. "Far from. But he did marry one." She lifted a fine brow. "Now you understand why I invited you."

"I might," he replied with a subtle grin. He'd suspected the evening would be rather interesting, but he was getting a sense he'd underestimated by a significant degree.

They were let into the house by a footman the size and approximate shape of a bull. Tall and solid with beefy shoulders and ham-sized fists. The grand entry hall was warm and welcoming, with gleaming parquet floors, rich mahogany wainscoting, and the scent of evergreen filling the air. Fresh boughs of Christmas greenery wound around the stairway banister and hung in heavy swags from the crown molding. Carefully placed candles lent a warm glow to the scene.

A very proper-looking butler greeted them next. After taking their outerwear, he led them to a well-lit drawing room, where festive ivy, holly, and mistletoe formed an enormous wreath trimmed with red ribbon that hung over the fireplace. Pausing in the doorway, the butler announced them as "Miss Callista Hale and guest, Mr. Erik Maxwell."

Callista. The name snaked delicately through Erik's mind. *Most beautiful.*

"Lissy!"

A great hulk of a man came striding forward, essentially blocking out the rest of the room and any other occupants from Erik's view. He was larger even than the footman had been, though with his long tawny hair falling loose about his shoulders and his muscled physique, he resembled a lion rather than a bull. It became apparent he was Pendragon's brother once Erik caught sight of the man's green eyes a few shades darker than hers. "I wasn't sure you'd come."

"I got the impression my attendance wasn't optional," she replied dryly.

Her brother flashed a wide grin. "It wasn't. But I'm still glad you made it." He leaned forward to mutter quietly, "It won't be as dreadful as you're thinking." Then he straightened and jerked his thumb in Erik's direction without bothering to look at him. "Who's this?"

The gesture told Erik a few things about the man; he had genuine affection for his sister and that included a protective streak that she either ignored or tolerated. And he was even more brash and crude than she ever allowed herself to be.

Pendragon slid him a sly glance from narrowed eyes. The corner of her mouth twisted upward as she replied, "This is Mr. Erik Maxwell. He owns a new gentleman's club in town and he's trying to seduce me."

Her brother gave rough snort as he flicked his glance to Erik. "Good luck with that, mate." The tone clearly indicated he expected abject failure, but he extended his hand and gave a firm handshake. "Mason Hale. Welcome."

"Thank you, Mr. Hale. I apologize for the intrusion."

Hale gave a shrug while a female voice spoke from behind him. "Not at all, Mr. Maxwell. We are quite happy to have you." A young woman with dark auburn hair and even darker brown eyes stepped around Hale's great form to offer a polite smile. Though she was nearly dwarfed by the man beside her, she possessed a quietly fierce presence that suggested she could hold her own against far more intimidating adversaries.

"My wife," Hale stated in a hard tone of warning as he slipped his arm around her slim waist. "Lady Katherine Hale."

Erik gave a proper bow. "A pleasure, my lady."

After giving a nod of acknowledgement, the young lady of the house turned her attention to Pendragon and stated with genuine feeling, "Thank you so much for joining us. The children will be down shortly. They were very much looking forward to your visit."

Looking back to Erik, she added with an arched brow, "I hope you have no aversion to the company of children, Mr. Maxwell."

"Of course not," he replied readily.

"Excellent. You'll likely discover our family prefers not to follow all the strict rules of social engagement."

"An understatement, luv," Hale muttered gruffly before pressing a kiss to his wife's temple. "You married me, after all."

The lady tossed him a glance of stern reprimand though her lips twitched with humor. Then she turned to gesture toward a seating arrangement placed before the room's enormous fireplace. "Please make yourselves comfortable."

"A drink, Lissy?" Hale asked as he started toward a liquor service in the corner.

Erik was surprised by her allowance of the nickname. He suspected that if Mr. Hale was subtly protective of his sister, then she was just as subtly indulgent of him.

"Claret, if you please."

"I'll have one, as well," Lady Katherine said as she led the way and took a graceful position in one of the tall wingback chairs.

"Maxwell?"

"The same. Thank you."

In an obviously contrary move, Pendragon claimed the other wingback chair in a flourish of her scarlet skirts, leaving the small settee for the men. Erik almost chuckled but managed to hold it in as he took a seat on one end of the narrow sofa. Leaning back, he crossed one ankle over the opposite knee. If the madam's intention was to make him uncomfortable, she'd have her work cut out for her. If his childhood performing in front of endless crowds taught him anything, it was how to avoid becoming distressed in even the most awkward circumstances.

Hale brought the ladies their wine first, then returned with a glass for Erik. It appeared he hadn't poured anything for himself. When he saw what the women had done, he made a low sound of displeasure. Sending his sister a swift glare, he took up a spot standing beside the fireplace, where the heat rolling from the roaring flames would likely soon grow unbearable.

Pendragon smirked in self-satisfaction as she sipped from her crystal wineglass.

"Are you only recently of London, Mr. Maxwell?" Lady Katherine asked.

He met the young woman's directly questioning gaze and noted that, although she wasn't as boldly beautiful as Madam Pendragon, there was a distinct loveliness in her dark eyes and fine features. "Yes, I arrived in England less than a year ago."

"And where were you before that?"

Her interest obviously derived from pure curiosity rather than a desire to pry, but Erik had to think on it for a moment. The extensive nature of his past travels tended to make the details blur together after a while. "I believe I was in Istanbul just prior to coming to London."

Lady Katherine's dark brows lifted in interest. "Really? Have you traveled to a great many places?"

Erik smiled. "More than I've time to name tonight, my lady."

"How fascinating. I've only ever been to Lincolnshire, where I grew up, and now London. I'd love to travel someday."

"We will, luv," Hale asserted firmly. "Once everything is settled. Promise."

His wife responded with a smile that reflected her complete and utter confidence in his words. Erik glanced to Pendragon, wondering if she saw the depth of faith and devotion between her brother and his wife. The Hales' marriage appeared to be a perfect example of what she claimed didn't exist.

Likely sensing his regard, she looked back at him. Her green eyes flashed with quiet frustration. When he tilted his head in silent question, she quickly averted her eyes and took another sip of her wine.

"Ah, here they are," Lady Katherine noted with a smile as she rose to her feet.

Erik stood as well and turned toward the doorway to see a dark-haired boy of twelve or thirteen holding the hand of a small girl with soft blonde curls who could be no more than three years old. The girl looked a bit shy as her blue eyes darted between Pendragon and Erik before settling on Hale.

"Come here, sweet pea," the big man said in a soft tone.

The girl immediately dashed forward to be swept up in Hale's arms.

"Frederick," Lady Katherine said as she gestured for the boy to come forward. "I'd like you to meet Mr. Maxwell. He is an associate of Miss Hale." Lifting her gaze to Erik, she continued, "Mr. Maxwell, this is my brother, the Duke of Northmoor."

After executing a bow appropriate for the boy's rank, Erik replied, "A pleasure to meet you, Your Grace."

With a surprisingly stoic expression for one so young and a sharply intelligent gaze, the young duke nodded. "And you, Mr. Maxwell. It is always nice to be introduced to new friends." Turning to Pendragon, he added, "I'm very happy to see you again, Miss Hale. Your visits always bring a welcome bit of excitement to the house."

Her smile was slightly teasing as she replied, "Then I shall do my best to come by more often."

"I think Claire would like that, as well," Hale interjected as he stepped forward with the little girl still held high in his thick arms. "Wouldn't you like to see Aunt Lissy more often, sweet pea?"

The little girl smiled sweetly and she nodded her head, causing her pale curls to bounce about her cheeks.

"See?" Hale stated emphatically as he gave his sister a smirking look.

She responded with a roll of her eyes.

Turning to Erik, Hale added, "And this is Aunt Lissy's friend, Mr. Maxwell."

Erik tilted his head toward the girl and offered a gentle smile. "A pleasure to meet you, Miss Claire."

After blushing prettily, she murmured softly, "Merry Christmas."

"And Merry Christmas to you."

"Well done, sweet pea," Hale whispered to the child as he set her down. The little girl went immediately to Lady Katherine, who scooped her up and placed her in her lap as she regained her seat.

Hale returned to his spot by the fireplace and the young duke took a seat on the settee next to Erik.

They continued to exchange small talk for a while. Lady Katherine questioned him a little further on his favorite places while Hale seemed intent on irritating his older sister. For her part, Pendragon appeared mostly relaxed, if a bit more restrained than he'd grown accustomed to seeing her. Likely, she was making an effort to hold back some of her more biting replies to her brother for the sake of the children. It became clear that Hale was fully aware of his sister's predicament and used it against her. She managed to say quite a lot, however, with her searing gaze, which only appeared to amuse Hale all the more.

At one point, while the children were busy on the other side of the room, admiring the snow falling outside the large bay window, her frustration finally got the better of her.

"Really, Mason, must you insist on calling me that dreadful nickname. I haven't been Lissy since you were a little brat who couldn't say my name properly."

Her brother simply grinned wide and teasing. "Sorry, sis. You'll always be Lissy to me."

Pendragon glanced to Lady Katherine. "How the hell do you put up with him?"

The lady arched her brow and slid the man under discussion a look that sparked with intimate heat before replying in a perfectly flat tone, "He's proven to have his uses."

Hale snorted a rough laugh, while Pendragon rose to her feet and smoothed the wrinkles from her gown. "Well, he certainly doesn't have much to offer in his head."

"Depends which you're referencing," Hale retorted crudely.

His sister responded with an exaggerated roll of her eyes. "If you'll excuse me. I'm in need of a brief respite from all this *family accord*."

As she swept from the room, Lady Katherine turned a harsh eye to her husband. "Do you always have to be so irritating? That's probably why she doesn't come by more often."

"You know that's not why and, yes, I do. My sister requires regular reminders that she belongs to a world that extends beyond the house off St. James." Turning to Erik, he added, "I'd guess Maxwell here knows what I mean."

He did but he knew better than to enter the fray.

"Could you at least try to make these rare visits more pleasant and enjoyable?" Lady Katherine pressed.

Hale shrugged, unconcerned. "If they were pleasant, she'd hate them even more."

Erik rose to his feet. "Please, excuse me." Leaving the couple to continue their argument without his audience, he left the drawing room and looked about the awe-inspiring entry hall. After a moment, he noticed a faint light visible beneath a door at the far end of the hall.

Walking quietly across the parquet floor, he opened the door without knocking.

Pendragon stood at the far end of the room, pouring herself a drink from a discreet liquor service. The room appeared to be a personal study containing a desk, some chairs, and a small sofa. As Erik approached, she glanced up with a visible frown before putting the stopper in the liquor bottle and lifting her glass to down its contents in one smooth swallow.

"Perhaps you missed my cue, Mr. Maxwell. I left the room to be alone."

Erik paused. "I do not wish to intrude. I just wanted to give your brother and his wife a few moments to finish a private conversation."

She smirked as she set her glass down and turned to face him while leaning back against the table behind her. "I assume they were arguing again. Those two have absolutely nothing in common. I cannot imagine why they thought it would be a good idea to marry."

Lifting a brow in genuine surprise, Erik continued forward until he stood directly in front of her. Close enough that her crimson skirts were stirred by his polished black boots. "Nothing in common?" He tilted his head to search her green eyes. Lowering his voice, he asked, "Surely you see the mutual respect and genuine admiration they have for each other. They are very different people with radically different backgrounds, I am sure. But they clearly appreciate those differences. I suspect they enjoy a deep abiding love."

Her eyes widened with mocking shock. "My God, you are utterly relentless and totally delusional."

He laughed. The woman fought hard to retain her skepticism. "If you did not see those things, surely you were able to detect the passion simmering between them."

"Passion is not love," she retorted curtly. "The hotter it burns, the faster it dies."

"When valued and properly nurtured, passion can richen and deepen with time."

"Passion is lust and lust weakens as soon as it's indulged."

Erik's gaze fell to her lips—reddened and lush. "Shall we test that theory?"

Boldly, irreverently, she tilted her head back and met his gaze with a challenging stare as she twisted her beautiful lips into an expression of sensual superiority. "Do your worst, Maxwell."

He could see in her eyes she expected to be disappointed. He couldn't allow that.

Stepping closer, he bracketed her feet with his, allowing his thighs to rest warmly against hers. Then he lifted a hand to her throat, caging the lengthened column with his fingers. The green of her eyes flashed brightly and her lips parted to allow a swift, subtle exhale. But beyond that, she did not react. He took a moment to meet her gaze, looking into her eyes with heavy intention, showing her what he wanted. Revealing the dark hunger in his soul and the secret yearning beneath the shadows.

As her eyes narrowed, shielding the flash of light he saw in their depths, he lowered his head and took her mouth in an instantly possessive kiss. The lush cushion of her lips—the spicy and unexpectedly sweet, heady taste of her—nearly distracted him from his purpose. Full, brutal honesty. Still holding her gaze, his hand remained secure around her throat as he swept his tongue past her teeth.

She answered the invasion with a short flick of her tongue against his. It was taunting and insolent. A reminder that she was no common conquest.

What she failed to accept was that Erik had never seen her as such. She was perfection in form. To him, she had already surpassed every prior lover he'd ever known. And there had been many...more, perhaps, than she even realized. At this moment, he only wanted her to know how deeply he wanted her and how badly he wished to please her.

He gave another long lick of his tongue within her mouth. It was wet and thick and unabashedly erotic and he was rewarded with a slight flutter of her sooty lashes and the darkening of her gaze.

Tilting his head, he fit his mouth more securely to hers. Gliding his tongue in and out until she responded with a languid swirl of her tongue past his lips. Taking advantage, he suckled her tongue, drawing it deeper into his mouth before releasing it. As her eyes finally fell closed, he nearly moaned but subdued the sense of triumph he felt at her subtle, momentary surrender. She was not a woman to remain submissive for long. He'd need every bit of his skill to show her why they shouldn't stop with a kiss.

He gave a brief and gentle squeeze of his hand at her throat, before sliding his fingers down over her collarbone, between her pushed-up breasts, to the inward curve of her waist. Grasping her in both hands, he brought her up against him—body to body—a stunning fit.

She seemed to agree as she brought her arms up around his neck and finally—fully—gave herself over to the kiss. Lips, tongue, teeth, breath. Swirling, tasting, licking, biting. It was passion and fire—a willful, intentional destruction, but he lost track of who was destroying whom as they went up in flames together.

Reminding himself of the need for patience in the midst of mindless desire, Erik finally pulled back, lifting his head enough to press a final kiss to the corner of her lush mouth.

A feeling unlike any he'd experienced before spread through him then as he slid his gaze over her features, noting the kohl-rimmed eyes, the fine cheekbones, and the way her lush, sensitive mouth curved just slightly downward at the corners. The sensation was bright and heady and wonderfully consuming.

As her eyes swept open, he felt a deep reluctance to let her go, even for the time being. A part of him feared she wouldn't let him this close again.

"We should return to our hosts," he said in a roughened voice.

She gave a short sound of derision. "Should we?"

He smiled at her show of scorn. "Though you sound put out, I suspect you fully enjoy their company. Even the children."

Pulling back from him, she smoothed her hands over her gown before replying, "One kiss and you presume to know what I enjoy."

Stepping closer to her, reclaiming the distance she'd placed between them, he replied in a heavy tone, "Your pleasure has become a part of me, madam. I cannot separate it from my own."

Though she arched her brow in a show of disdain, her pulse fluttered at the side of her throat and her gaze slipped briefly to his mouth before she replied coolly, "I hope that doesn't prove too painful for you." Then she swept past him and left the room.

The damned woman was forever walking away from him.

It was his greatest desire to change that.

Chapter Seven

Dinner was called shortly after their return to the party and they all moved into the dining room. It was a formal, imposing space with a grand table that could easily seat a dozen or more. More richly scented evergreen formed a simple but festive centerpiece. The winter greenery was accented with red ribbons, glossy apples, and bright oranges.

The children remained with them through dinner. Having Frederick and Claire at the table assisted in lightening and enlivening the tone of the evening, giving it a casual feel despite the obvious care that had gone into the exceptional meal consisting of various roasted meats, seasoned vegetables, mincemeat pies, steamy sweet breads, and Christmas puddings soaked in brandy.

The young Duke of Northmoor was exceptionally intelligent and well-versed in various topics of conversation. He contributed to the adult conversation with as much ease and seriousness as he used when he spoke quietly with young Claire. At one point, Lady Katherine explained that the two of them had grown up under rather unusual circumstances. Their mother had died when they were young and their father had been intensely devoted to his work in the field of herbalism and pharmacology, leaving his children to form their own educations and far from the influence most often forced upon aristocratic children to meet a certain molded expectation.

"And I'm damned grateful, for it brought you stumbling through my door," Hale added as he took his wife's hand and brought it to his lips.

"Stumbling?" the lady asked with a haughtily raised brow. "I believe you've forgotten that our first encounter involved a set of dueling pistols aimed for your person."

"On the contrary, it's one of my favorite memories," he murmured thickly before giving a quick wink that brought a tint of pink to her cheeks.

Erik glanced to Callista with a lifted brow, wondering if she'd concede his earlier point. But she appeared to have missed the interaction between her brother and his wife as she was busy staring at him instead. Her expression was tense and her gaze narrowed as though she were contemplating something intently.

He suspected he knew exactly what was on her mind.

The kiss they'd shared had been everything he'd known it would be—intense and erotic, but also undeniably emotional. He'd hazard a guess to say it might have been a bit more than she'd expected.

There was no hiding from the passion between them. The *potential*. Only a fool would deny it existed and the woman was no fool. Despite that, Erik was under no delusion that his campaign had been won with a single kiss.

As her gaze flickered with the shadow of something unnamed, he almost wished he could reassure her. But she'd have to come to her own conclusions about what she was feeling and what it meant for the two of them.

Though he chose not to say anything, he did offer a smile.

Her expression tightened in response before she looked away to sip from her wineglass.

After the meal, the party returned to the drawing room. It wasn't much longer before Claire's nurse came to fetch the young girl. Though she pouted about having to leave, it was clear the little girl was ready for bed. The young duke decided to go upstairs as well. Though his sister assured he could stay and visit a bit longer if he liked, he explained that he wished to work on his current project before going to bed. Before they left, Callista stopped the children beside her chair. Leaning toward them, she whispered something and handed each of them a small velvet pouch. Their smiles were bright as they continued from the room.

"That wasn't necessary, Lissy."

There was a heavy note in Hale's voice, but his sister looked at him with an arched brow. "It was just a few sweets and a coin or two. Nothing inappropriate, I assure you."

"Still a helluva lot more than we ever got," he muttered gruffly.

"Yes, well, that is the whole point, isn't it, Mace? To leave the evils of the past in the gin-soaked lanes where they belong."

A silent communication passed between the siblings before Hale raised his glass. "Hear, hear." After that, he launched into a tale of one particular holiday in his youth that involved a runaway pig, a gang of street urchins, and a frozen ditch that proved to be not so frozen after all. Erik followed with a story of one year when his acting troupe met up with a caravan of the Rom while traveling through Italy. The two groups all contributed to an elaborate festival of dancing, drinking, and feasting that lasted four days without stop.

The evening continued with more shared stories and bittersweet recollections as laughter flowed as freely as the wine. Eventually, however, the hour grew late and the liveliness of the gathering began to fade. As they all made their way to the entry hall, where the butler waited to hand off their winter coats and cloaks, Hale hauled Lady Katherine in against his side with a thick arm around her waist. Tossing his sister a wide grin, he said, "Not such a bad evening, eh, Lissy?"

The look she gave him was full of amiable annoyance. "It was tolerable, I suppose."

Lady Katherine, not at all put out by Callista's sarcastic response, smiled warmly. "I thought it was lovely. Thank you both so much for celebrating the holiday with us. I hope we'll have an opportunity to repeat the experience soon."

Erik was in the process of settling Callista's black fur-lined cloak about her shoulders and he felt the brief, subtle tensing in her body. Smoothing his hands over her shoulders, he replied to their hostess with an easy smile. "It would be a pleasure and an honor, Lady Katherine."

The night was crisp with cold, but the sky was clear. Moonlight and stars brightened the sky and filtered a silver haze into the atmosphere as they climbed into the carriage, where a warmer had been set on the floor to keep their toes from freezing. Even so, Erik immediately reached for the heavy woolen rugs set in the corner and unfolded them over their legs.

Though they sat close beside each other to share the limited warmth, neither spoke for a while as their breath puffed cold into the air. And when he noticed the woman beside him still shivering with cold even after the vehicle began to warm, he brought his arm up around her shoulders and slowly drew her in closer against his side.

If she had given any sign of resistance to the shift in position, he would have ceased, but she didn't. In fact, she offered a quiet sigh as she rested her head against his shoulder and curved her body toward his. One of her hands fell to his upper thigh beneath the blanket, causing a swift rise in his internal temperature.

With his cock hardening and his chest aching sweetly, he looked down to see that her eyes had closed and her features were in repose. He wasn't sure if it was the wine or their shared comfort that encouraged her to claim a moment of rest, but he was grateful for it as he allowed himself the luxury of admiring her beauty at this intimate angle.

The black kohl lining her eyes added a dramatic element to her features but he found himself more mesmerized by the lush fan of her lashes against her smooth skin. The red tint she often added to her generously curved lips had all but faded away throughout the evening, leaving her mouth a dusky rose color that was soft and sensual. Even in repose, there was an element of calculated ambition in the details of her face. It was there in her broad, smooth forehead and in the angled, almost square shape of her jaw and in the slashing arches of her elegant brows.

Such a formidable woman.

He knew she could be ruthless when it was warranted. She could be cool and manipulative and brash. She was relentlessly competitive and arrogant and utterly bewitching. And yet, she was allowing this moment. A moment of silent companionship and shared ease.

His heart ached with the privilege even as his body tensed and hardened with the visceral pleasure of having her lush softness pressed against him.

Leaning his head back against the wall of the carriage, he closed his eyes, as well. Listening to her even breath and the rhythm of the carriage wheels while soaking up the warmth and ease and honor of holding her in his arms, he might have drifted off a bit before the lurch of the vehicle as it came to a stop brought him swiftly back to full awareness. Blinking, he lifted his head and glanced about as the lady in his arms also stirred. Her hand on his thigh tensed and squeezed as she used it to leverage herself to a more independently seated position a moment before the groom opened the carriage door.

As she leaned forward to glance outward, she muttered a quiet curse.

"What is the matter?" Erik looked past her into the night. Beyond the groom who stood holding the door, he saw a softly lit townhouse. The residence was stately and stylish in a way that spoke of understated wealth.

"I forgot to instruct the driver to drop you at your club."

"Where are we?" He knew it wasn't Pendragon's Pleasure House as he'd already made sure to acquaint himself with its location though not its services.

Her expression tightened as she replied in a clipped tone, "I'd prefer no one know of this place."

"Your private residence?"

"Private no longer, unfortunately," she grumbled in response.

"It pleases me to know you have a place you can go to retreat from all of the demands on your time and personal attention," he replied gently.

He waited for her to say that it was not her intention to please him, but she just slid him a glance from the corner of her eye and said nothing.

"I'm sure you're anxious to be in the warmth and comfort of your home. I'll walk you to your door, then your driver can take me to my club."

"No," she replied readily, "you can stay here, I'll walk myself to the door, then my driver can take you to your club."

Erik laughed. "As you wish, madam, but first..." He caught her gaze with his. "I must request another kiss."

Her lips curled in amusement. "You *must*?"

"Indeed," he replied, lowering his voice to an intimate murmur. "If I did not, I would never forgive myself for the cowardice of letting you go without at least *trying* to taste you again."

Cynicism returned to her gaze. "And why should I allow it this time?"

"Because you want to taste me just as badly. And you are no more a coward than I am."

Her laugh was sultry but held a harsh note. "You think that kind of blatant challenge will work on me?"

"I do. Because it is the simple truth."

He waited for her acknowledgement, knowing it would come. Because along with her bold confidence came deep and undeniable self-awareness. He saw the acceptance in her eyes a moment before she placed her hand back on his thigh and leaned toward him.

Lifting his gloved hand, he slid his fingers along the side of her jaw then back to curve around the base of her skull and gently tip her face up to his. Tension built between them as he stared into her eyes before moving to take her mouth.

She likely expected a kiss similar to their first—fiery and fierce. But he wanted something else in this moment. Wanted to *offer* something else.

As a gust of frigid air swept through the open door of the carriage, causing the woman in his arms to give a delicate shudder, he lowered his head. Brushing his lips warmly across her cool lips in a careful application of friction and pressure, he waited for her eyes to drift closed. As soon as they did, he began to sip gently from her lips in quiet little kisses.

Her soft sigh as her mouth parted urged him to deepen the kiss. Adjusting his hand to more fully cup the back of her head, he angled his mouth over hers. Though their lips were parted enough to share warmth of breath, he did not employ his tongue to taste her secrets just yet.

The slow seduction of the kiss affected him as much as he hoped it might affect her. His insides melted with yearning and desire. His body thrummed with need. But it was a need he was more than happy to deny. The pleasure to be found in the lush sweetness of her mouth was all he wanted to explore just now.

Her hand shifted on his thigh as she leaned farther into him, her breasts pressing to his chest. There was no stopping the low growl of hunger that rumbled in his throat as he brought his other arm around her back to hold her against him as he finally slipped his tongue between her lips to deepen the kiss.

Her response was languid and perfect. An answering twirl of her tongue against his, then a nip on his lower lip when he withdrew.

They opened their eyes at the same time and Erik slowly eased his hold from around her body. But before she could fully retreat from him, he asked roughly, "When shall I see you again?"

Something flashed in her gaze, something that caused a clench of concern.

Pulling free of his arms, she turned toward the carriage door. "I'll be rather busy for a while."

The groom assisted her from the vehicle but Erik couldn't leave it at that. Before she could walk away from him yet again, he leaned forward to remind her, "There are six days remaining in our agreement."

Wrapping her cloak securely around herself, she looked at him over her shoulder and offered a sly, knowing smile. "That is true, but I am a busy woman, Mr. Maxwell. Something of which you are well aware. I will not change my life to suit your purposes."

He frowned. "And I would never ask you to." Her devotion to her business was one of the things he admired most about her. And the truth was, if he could not convince her to give him a chance within the boundaries she had set, then he did not deserve her time.

She arched her brows. "Wouldn't you?"

The distrust in her voice struck him harder and deeper than ever before. He'd thought she was starting to understand him as he was coming to better understand her. He'd hoped she might be starting to feel some real affection for him.

But as she turned away and walked to the front door of her private residence, he realized he might be further from his goal than he'd thought.

Chapter Eight

Callista rarely made mistakes when it came to Pendragon's. She took risks on occasion and experimented every once in a while, but she never considered any of her decisions—even those that did not turn out as well as expected—*mistakes*.

But the moment she dropped the invitation in the post, she suspected she'd made the biggest mistake of her life.

Yet she refused to take the small missive back.

Callista was nothing if not honest with herself.

She was fully aware that she had spent the last couple decades obsessively focused on creating a business and a life that could not be compromised by any man.

She knew she'd sacrificed a great many personal relationships to achieve her goal, though she'd managed to somehow tenuously hold on to the only one that really mattered. Even that, she acknowledged, was likely due more to Mason's efforts than her own.

She was driven, ambitious, focused, and maybe a little preoccupied with attaining personal power. But she also knew those things were motivated by a past when she'd had nothing, and the sense of powerlessness she'd experienced had nearly ruined her.

She also had to admit to herself that she had enjoyed Christmas this year more than any year prior and it had been all because of the company.

So, if she could recognize and accept her faults and occasionally flawed motivations, she had to also admit when something she'd assumed to be fact turned out to be incorrect.

Erik Maxwell and his gentleman's club, or whatever it was, did not pose any threat to Pendragon's Pleasure House. They might cater to a similar social demographic, but any gentleman interested in the pleasures offered by her establishment would not be the same type of man who sought entrance to Maxwell's. Her time with the man had convinced her that if nothing else, he believed whole-heartedly in what he was doing. And because of that, there was no need to drive him out of town.

No need to deny her intense attraction to the man and resist his seduction any longer.

If she weren't so accustomed to redirecting men's desires and resisting their attempts at influencing her, she would have tossed herself into Maxwell's bed the night they'd shared the brandy in front of his fire.

But the truth was, in the spirit of being completely honest with herself, Callista also had to admit that her feelings for the man were far more complicated than simple lust.

Somehow, he'd managed to slip beneath her barriers. With his smooth words and intense gaze, he'd accessed parts of her she'd long ago learned to keep hidden. She could deny it all she wanted to his face, but he'd been absolutely correct about the fact that there was a part of her she hadn't allowed past Pendragon's façade in a long time. He'd seen it and he'd delicately trailed his fingertips along her sensitive and vulnerable underbelly.

With his patient questions and quiet consideration and the way he seemed to genuinely want to know the contents of her mind as much as he wanted to release the contents of her corset, he'd ignited a few secret wishes she'd tucked so far into the shadows of her being, she'd forgotten they existed.

And now that they'd been relit, she couldn't ignore them.

In fact, she suspected she might want to explore them. Even if it were for only one night. She simply couldn't allow any more than that. But a lot could happen in one night.

AFTER WEEKS OF PREPARATION, Pendragon's annual end-of-the-year celebration event had finally arrived.

Callista always took exceptional and deliberate care with her appearance, but on this night it felt different. Because she wasn't dressing to stun and awe the dozens of high-spenders who'd be coming to Pendragon's expecting a night of exceptional pleasures and over-the-top depravities. She was dressing for one man only.

Keeping in line with her signature red and black, the dress she wore tonight was one she'd designed herself. The base of the gown was a blood-red silk, but instead of the empire waist currently in fashion, the bodice was designed into a full corset that shaped her figure from breasts to hips. Delicate swaths of silk draped over her shoulders, leaving her arms bare and her dragon on full display. There would be no gloves tonight.

The skirts of the gown had been slit in several places from the hem, all the way up to the embroidered base of her corset, revealing an underskirt of black lace. As she walked and moved, the transparent lace would be revealed, showing suggestive glimpses of her bare legs beneath.

But only glimpses.

Her slippers were black beaded satin and a black onyx choker encircled her throat. In her elaborately styled hair were several red roses so dark they appeared almost black in certain light.

She looked magnificent.

Strong. Seductive. Utterly in command and utterly untouchable by the common man.

It was the persona she'd spent years creating, and tonight, she was at the height of her power.

Pendragon's Pleasure House was located near St. James Square and Mayfair, where so many of the high-society gentlemen she catered to lived in domestic dissatisfaction. Decorated entirely in a Grecian theme, the larger rooms held mural-sized paintings depicting blatant sexual scenes, and marble pillars framed every doorway. The main floor contained an entry hall where her doormen carefully managed the flow of people entering and exiting the building. Even on regular nights, one must either be on the list of established members, be sponsored by an approved member in high esteem, or they must have a direct invitation from Pendragon herself. Once allowed in, guests could wander through various public rooms, each one leading deeper into the heart of the house where hedonistic sin and wickedness reigned.

Music played by five musicians flowed from the grand salon, which also contained a stage for her dancers surrounded by chairs, sofas, couches, and divans for comfortable viewing of the entertainment and other activities. A second salon had been designed more for conversation, where gentlemen could debate over port and tobacco while naked lovelies served them from golden platters. Beyond that was a room lit with soft candlelight, most often occupied by those who wished to engage in exhibitionism or voyeurism. And then, a room left in perpetual shadowed darkness to allow guests to release their inhibitions to the full extent. Alcoholic refreshment was provided in each room while light and savory fare was offered in the main drawing room to keep guests from leaving to pursue dinner elsewhere.

Several rooms on the upper floors were dedicated to Pendragon's personal use. Additional rooms were reserved for her ladies. She currently had nine in residence, though she hired additional entertainment for special events like tonight. For that purpose, several additional private rooms could be used as needed. Every available bed, couch, divan, and chaise in the place would likely be occupied well into the morning hours.

She'd thrown enough of these grand parties by now to have it all organized to perfection. The cellar and larders were well-stocked. Extra servants filled the kitchens and below stairs to keep everything moving smoothly and she had double her usual flash men to keep her guests in line should the excessive alcohol lead to any behavior that broke the strict house rules. One misdeed could see a member barred for life, which meant there were rarely infractions and events such as these tended to go off without a hitch.

Waiting until the evening was in full swing before leaving her rooms to join the party so as to make the kind of dramatic entrance she was known for, Callista sauntered down the main staircase in full view of the entry hall and the main salon.

She loved this moment.

When all eyes turned to her. Admiration, lust, and a little bit of fear reflected up at her. This was her world and she was empress. The lady dragon ready to bestow her treasures on foolish mortals or send them to fiery fates.

As she scanned the crowd below with a narrowed gaze, she exalted in her success. *She* had made this. With her wits and determination. She was far more than a vessel for men's pleasure. She was a force. Though she did not immediately see silver-streaked black hair or striking gray eyes amongst the gathering guests, she was not concerned.

He would come.

With a smile full of knowledge and secrets, she wove a seductive dance through the crowd. Bestowing grace upon her guests with a glance, a few words, or—if the gentleman were particularly lucky that evening—a light, suggestive caress of her hand as she passed. Each man held his breath, hoping they might be one to receive some exceptional favor from the queen of the evening. Callista very carefully and intentionally cultivated that hopeful anticipation. Part of her allure was in her unpredictability, the way her mood could shift from hot to cold and back again within a single interaction. It kept the gentlemen on their toes, never certain of her regard, ever aware of how much power she possessed within the walls of Pendragon's and beyond.

Their pleasures relied upon her grace and discretion and she made sure they never forgot that.

After taking a couple hours to make her way through each room, assessing the turnout and verifying that her protections were all in place should a guest get unruly, she went below stairs to check on things in the kitchen and go over additional details for the evening with her manager. Neither of which were necessary, as everything had been planned and prepped to perfection.

As she returned to the main level, she advised her head doorman that she would be in her personal suite if anything was needed. She liked to show herself only sparingly to her guests though she'd remain available for any concerns throughout the event. It was important she keep herself at a distance. Too much familiarity bred confidence and comfort, which led some men to think they could take more than they were offered, that they were somehow *owed* more.

Those men quickly learned otherwise.

Retreating to her library, her favorite room in the house, Callista poured herself a glass of red wine before reclining on her black velvet chaise.

Tonight would be a success. All of her grand parties were though each one became more elaborate than the last as she was forced over and over to outdo herself.

A glance at the clock indicated it was already early morning, yet the revelry and debauchery would continue for several more hours.

Leaning her head back, she closed her eyes. Anyone who might happen to observe her in that moment would assume she was resting. They'd be wrong.

Her body was taut with anticipation, which had been increasing throughout the day and evening. And her mind whirled through thoughts that were unprecedented.

Thoughts of a man who'd claimed her focus and her desire. A man she no longer believed to be a threat to her business, though he most certainly posed a significant risk to her personally.

In business she had always been fearless.

But in this...she had to acknowledge she'd become slightly unsteady.

It had been a long time since her last lover. But that was not what had her belly trembling at the thought of welcoming Erik Maxwell to her bed. What bothered her and threw her off-balance tonight was the realization and acceptance that what she wanted from him was different from anything she'd wanted before.

"Madam."

She opened her eyes without lifting her head to see one of her well-trained men filling the doorway. "Yes?"

"Your special guest has arrived."

Tingling, sparking anticipation rushed through her from head to toe. "Thank you, Simon."

With a nod, the bouncer stepped back into the hall and disappeared.

Sipping on her wine, Callista allowed a smile.

Of course he'd come.

No doubt, he was grateful for the opportunity to explore Pendragon's while also expecting to take advantage of her invitation to further his seduction. She hadn't seen him since Christmas dinner, yet per their agreement, he still had two days to demonstrate his skills. He couldn't know that, after tonight, they would no longer be needed.

Though a part of her wanted to rush downstairs to him, she forced herself to remain where she was. She wanted to allow him time to wander about and soak up the fantasy she'd woven for her guests.

What would he find most compelling?

Her stomach tightened. Would he choose to partake in the many wicked delights Pendragon's offered in abundance?

The urge to claim him for her own rose fiercely inside her. Now that she'd embraced the decision to accept him as her lover, she had to fight against a sense of possession. He did not belong to her any more than she would belong to him. No matter how intensely she was compelled to claim that right.

She paused in the midst of lifting her glass for another sip as a distinguished male form clothed in elegant black evening wear that accented the silver of his hair and the magnetic light in his eyes moved into the open doorway.

He stood there for a moment as his steady focused gaze moved slowly over the curves and dips of her body showcased to perfection by blood-red silk.

Though she felt the heat of his desire like flames licking over her skin, she responded to his appearance with a lift of her brow. Rolling to one side, she propped herself up on an elbow and noted smoothly, "The party is downstairs."

"I'm not here for the party." Understated confidence flowed through his words. And hunger. Heavy, rich hunger.

For the first time, she allowed some of her own hunger to reflect in her eyes. "I hope you allowed yourself a moment to take in the various delights I offer my guests."

He took a slow step into the room, then another. His gaze never leaving hers as he crossed the thick carpet. "What I want isn't being offered below."

"Is that so?" she asked with a quirk of her lips.

His smile was slow. Assured. Seductive. Did he already suspect why he'd been invited tonight?

"You know it is," he replied.

"What else do I know?"

Reaching the chaise, he extended one of his gloveless hands.

There was no hesitation as she slid her bare fingers along his palm until his hand enclosed hers and he brought her slowly to her feet. Without a word, he took her wineglass and set it on the table beside them. Then he lifted her hand to his mouth, where he pressed his warm lips to the center of her palm.

His silvery eyes held a quiet, unshakeable intention. But it was unhurried and calm. So unlike the riot erupting in her core. A part of her wanted him to sweep her off her feet, maybe toss her over his shoulder or take her to the floor right there in the middle of her library as he covered her mouth in a deep, claiming kiss. But another part of her held her breath and urged her to patience.

His voice was gruff and weighted when he finally replied. "You had to know I would find you."

She hadn't, actually. But she realized now that she'd hoped he would.

"Just as you know I am about to kiss you."

Callista lifted her chin as her lashes swept over a narrowed gaze and her lips parted. She felt no need to respond as his attention fell from her eyes to her mouth. She watched with thrills livening her blood as his pupils dilated and his nostrils flared.

Take it. The private thought came out in a husky murmur she hadn't intended to voice out loud. But then she was glad she did because a gravelly moan rolled from his throat as he took her face in his hands and claimed her mouth in a kiss that was deep, hot, and mind-melting.

As she slid one hand up and around his neck, she flattened her other palm to his chest, seeking the subtle rhythm of his heart as she gave herself over to the delicious skill he employed with his lips, tongue, and teeth. He immediately shifted to wrap his arms fully around her, one bracing behind her shoulders, the other encircling the narrow span of her tightly corseted waist to hold her close. Body to body. Breath to breath.

As hot as the kiss was to start, it grew even hotter. The flames of long-denied desire leaping to new heights within seconds.

Just when she thought she might drown in the maelstrom of need flowing through her, he slid his mouth to the side of her throat, then lower, where he paused to scrape his teeth delicately along the muscle connecting neck to shoulder before he placed a warm kiss just above the draping, wispy sleeve of her gown. The delicate caress caused shivers to cascade down her spine.

The hand she'd been resting against his chest curled into claws and her fingernails dug into the expensive fabric of his coat.

Lifting his head, he rested his mouth against the sensitive shell of her ear. "Most importantly," he whispered roughly, "you know the one thing I do not."

"What's that?" she asked. Her voice breathless and heavy.

"What happens next."

She opened her eyes to find him staring intently at her face. His eyes were hard and hot. His jaw was tense with need, his lips firm, and his breath subtly ragged.

"But you've known what would happen all along, Mr. Maxwell."

"I've hoped."

She smiled and combed her fingers through the hair at his nape. "Hmm. Now, you play at humility," she murmured thoughtfully.

He smiled but the curve of his mouth did nothing to soften the intensity in his expression. "Only an idiot would be anything but humble in the presence of the lady dragon."

The sound she made was a warm purr. "And you are no idiot."

His hands shifted to grasp her waist. She could feel the tension of his fingers pressing into the stiff material of her bodice, as if he wished to tear it away from her body to reach the softness encased within.

She wanted to tear the damn thing off, just to feel the smooth glide of his bare hands on her skin. Instead, she gave a subtle undulation of her body. A quiet urging, a silent permission for him to take a bit more.

Eyes blazing, he smoothed his hands up along her sides until his thumbs brushed across the peaks of her breasts with the perfect amount of pressure before he reached around her. One hand slid down to press flat against the lowest curve of her spine, right where her buttocks flared beneath soft silk. His other hand followed her spine up to wrap around her nape. Holding her like that, he brushed a light kiss across her parted lips.

"I'm clever enough to know my first mistake with you would also be my last."

"You think me so harsh?" she asked in a ragged whisper as his lips trailed to her jaw, then her temple, then the hollow below her ear.

"Not harsh, madam. You are simply too magnificent for most mortal men."

She gave a husky laugh. The man knew how to compliment a woman.

His hand tightened on the back of her neck, urging her to drop her head, exposing her throat. She expected him to kiss her there. Instead, he held her like that for a moment. Just long enough for vulnerability to spark deep in her heart. But as she met his dynamic gaze, swirling with desire and knowledge, she instinctively knew she was safe in his hold.

"But I am not most men."

She narrowed her focus on his mouth, admiring its firm lines and the softness that was present only in the fuller bottom lip. She ached for that mouth and its unexpected smiles and intriguing words. She trembled inside with the desire to feel it again on her lips and imagined the many other ways he might use it.

Bringing her gaze back to his, she murmured in agreement, "No. You are not."

Chapter Nine

When she stepped from his arms, Erik experienced a moment of panic but loosened his hold anyway, allowing his hands to glide over her curves in a sensual caress that made her eyes spark beautifully and her lips curve with promise.

Then she took his hand in hers and turned to lead him across the room. Without a word, she continued from the library and down the hall toward the rear of the house, away from the main stairs that that would have taken them back down to the party. Next, they ascended a narrow, twisting staircase to the top floor of the building and another hallway with red carpeting and brocade-covered walls that contained several closed doors.

Despite the muffled sounds of revelry that could be heard from below and the suspicion that there were others enjoying the privacy and quiet behind each of the closed doors they passed, he felt as though it were just the two of them. In the world that surrounded them but not *of* it. He always seemed to feel like that when he was with her.

At the end of the hall was a door, closed and locked.

Sending him a seductive glance over her shoulder that had his stomach tightening and his cock thickening in a rush, she withdrew a single key on a silken black cord from a concealed pocket in her gown.

The room beyond was a luxurious sitting room done in more of the lady's signature scarlet but accented with gold rather than black. Gold threads in the embroidered settee, gold in the flames rolling gently in the hearth, gold brocade drapes covering the windows, and a large gold filigreed mirror on the wall between.

The room was gilded fire.

And as Pendragon led the way forward, he acknowledged how perfect a setting it was for her. He couldn't keep his eyes off her in the stunning gown, her hips swaying confidently beneath liquid flowing silk. Closing the door behind him, he leaned back against it, watching her. Admiring everything about her as she stopped in front of the oversized mirror hanging almost directly across the room from him.

Green eyes snared his in the reflection as she lifted her hands to tuck a stray curl back up into her coiffure. Her smile was full of feminine mystique and sensual power as she allowed her fingertips to trail slowly down along her slim neck, across her collarbone, and lower, to the soft upper swells of her breasts.

As he watched from behind her, the mirrored reflection making him feel farther away than he was in truth, she slid her index finger along the top of her bodice, where a thin edge of black lace peeked from under the red silk.

Lust swirled heavily in his body, tensing his muscles, clenching a fist around his throat while blood thundered to his cock.

The woman could put him to his knees if she tried. Part of him wished she would. He would readily offer every pleasure to her, prostrate himself at her feet for the privilege of a single taste.

But he understood that wasn't what she wanted. Nor was it what she needed. She'd no doubt had countless men bowing to her beauty and her pleasure, tossing themselves at the mercy of her desires.

Their intense mutual attraction had grown into something far more complex than sexual power dynamics and pleasures of the flesh alone. He'd long accepted the connection between them. The inevitability of their joining and the undeniable enjoyment that would be found when they finally came together. As two people who might appear to be rivals on the outside but were well-matched in all the ways that mattered.

Their pasts had been charted through decades of experiences and ambitions and loneliness to bring them both to this night. To each other.

Her fingers moved nimbly along the tiny hidden fasteners running down the front of her gown. With each little pop of the hook releasing from eyelet, the stiff bodice began to gape.

And Erik's mouth began to water.

Lush, pale pink flesh. Soft and full. She wore nothing beneath the gown and every bit she exposed to him was more tantalizing than the last. As his gaze hungrily devoured the sensual feast she revealed so cleverly and torturously, he felt as though he were being offered something no man could ever prove worthy of receiving.

Pulling the corseted bodice free of her body, she dropped the thing to the floor.

The smooth skin of her torso gleamed like marble in the dusky golden firelight. Her breasts were wonderfully full, the tips crested with dark rose-colored nipples. Her waist was narrow but soft in a way he wanted to rub his face against.

Still facing the mirror and now bared from waist up, she reached behind her back to where a tied ribbon secured the skirts around her narrow waist. The position thrust her breasts higher, making them jiggle delightfully.

Reluctantly lifting his gaze from her creamy bosom, he noted the small tilt of a satisfied smile curling her mouth. The consummate seductress. Her sexual assurance was intoxicating, leaving him incapable of doing anything but staring with clenched teeth.

Understanding his predicament entirely, she gave a soft chuckle before pulling the ribbon of her skirts, freeing the red silk to fall in a billowy scarlet cloud to the floor.

A powerful jolt of need shot through him. But he forced himself to remain unmoving.

Clad only in an underskirt of transparent black lace that did next to nothing to conceal the lush flare of her hips or the long lines of her shapely legs, she turned to face him. The shadow of pale gold curls at the juncture of her thighs nearly did him in.

With herculean effort, he swallowed the deep groan of hunger pushing up from his chest and managed to utter three true words. "You slay me."

A blonde brow arced. "Isn't that what dragons do? Surely, you didn't expect me to spare you my flames."

"I'd willingly drown in your fire. But I'd prefer we dance in the flames together."

Sparks lit her gaze as she started toward him. Slowly but with undeniable purpose. Her steps languid. The movement of her body sultry. Sensual confidence flowed through her form, holding her shoulders back as her hips swayed.

Stopping halfway across the room, she lowered her chin and smiled with sinful promise as she beckoned him with a curl of her finger.

Pushing off from the door, he reached her in long, swift strides. He saw her ribs expand and her full breasts lift with a swift inhale that caught and held. Her kohl-rimmed eyes were narrowed and dark, watching him. Her reddened lips slightly parted to show the edge of white teeth.

Though his hands burned with the desire to smooth over her pale skin, to cover her breasts and pinch their peaks, he instead reached up to gently caress one of the roses in her hair.

Petals like the richest velvet. A red so dark it was nearly black. And as he carefully withdrew the first bloom from her golden tresses, he discovered the stem still held its thorns.

He took care releasing her twisted and curled coiffure, making sure not to tug too hard on the pins or tangle the blooms in his attempt to free them. Within minutes, her hair fell in long gilded waves to her hips, framing her stunning beauty in pale gold light.

His chest tightened as the fierce fire of possession engulfed him. "Callista."

Her given name slipped from his lips on a ragged whisper before he could hold it back. Her eyes flashed, but she said nothing.

She was a creature beyond fantasy. An ancient and sensual goddess. A woman of myth and magic. And tonight she was his.

Still holding the last rose he'd slipped from her hair—a full-blown bloom with wicked thorns and a scent of sensual promise so intoxicating it made his head spin—Erik lifted the flower to brush the petals softly across her lips. Though he felt her gaze intent upon his face, he couldn't keep from watching the path of the rose as he trailed it down the side of her neck, along her collarbone, then down between the heavy globes of her breasts to her navel. Circling the rose over her low belly, he watched her muscles tense with a satisfied smile.

Drawing the rose up again, he followed the undercurve of one breast. Her nipples tightened and puckered beneath his gaze, anticipating the velvet touch of the rose.

Tension rode gently across her brow as breath passed swiftly between her lips and her green eyes flashed.

Had the bewitching seductress finally fallen under his spell?

Holding her gaze, he circled the peak of first one breast, then the other. Her lashes fluttered as she spoke in a husky whisper. "Beware how much you tease. I've some skill in sensual torment, as well."

"I fucking hope so," he replied in a gravelly confession, drawing a soft chuckle from her throat.

He took that moment to lower his head and take one breast fully in his mouth, drawing the budded peak deep.

Her gasp was loud and raw as her hands lifted to grasp his head and her spine arched.

Slipping one arm around her waist, he held her secure to accept the luscious roll of his tongue and the sharp edge of his teeth. Her body fit perfectly within the concave curve of his. Their legs intertwined, her low belly was soft against his aching erection, and her breasts lifted to his mouth. When he turned his head to capture the other breast for equal attention, her fingers curled into his hair, tugging at the scalp while holding him to her.

She knew her pleasure and how to claim it.

But he wanted to give her more. More than she'd ever experienced. More than she knew was possible. He was offering all that he was to this woman tonight. Every breath and thunderous beat of his heart.

Grabbing her buttocks in his hands, he raised his head and lifted her against him. Her legs parted to wrap around his hips.

"Bed?" The one word was a question and a demand.

"Through the door behind you," she gasped before rolling her hips along his length.

His grip on her lush rear tightened as he turned in place. If he didn't hurry, they wouldn't make it to a bed, and he so wanted to have her spread out on the softness of a mattress as he attended to her pleasure.

The room beyond was dark compared to the outer room, but after only a moment, his eyes began to adjust to the dim, seductive candlelight.

The bedroom was small, and if the sitting room had been gilded fire, this room was all secret darkness and wicked night. The walls were black and silver brocade and thick black carpeting covered the floor. The four-poster bed was made of wood that gleamed a cherry red in the candlelight and was dressed in velvets the color of a midnight sky. But in the center of the room was a straight chaise bench, long and wide, covered in sleek red leather that no doubt felt like butter to touch.

The chaise gave him ideas. Sinfully delicious ideas.

Later.

He took her first to the bed, but he didn't lay her down. Instead, he lowered her feet to the floor and pressed her back to the bedpost behind her. Their gazes locked and held, but neither of them spoke. He could feel her expectation, her trust—if only in this—as she appeared content in the moment to await his direction.

Grasping her wrists in his hands, he lifted them up over her head until she wrapped her elegant fingers around the smooth column of the bedpost. Then he slid her hands higher. Higher. Until she was stretched out, reaching far above her head, elongating her torso, and lifting her plump breasts.

Erik stepped back to admire the picture she made. Skin pale in the darkness, the swirl of black lace shielding her lower body, her gaze direct and challenging, her lips red and glistening.

"Gorgeous."

His low murmured word sounded like a benediction in the dark silence.

Utterly fitting as he lowered to his knees before her. She still wore her black heeled slippers. He left them in place as he smoothed his hands up the outsides of her legs, reaching beneath the fall of lace. Taking a deep breath, he drew in the rich, honied scent of her as he explored the silk of her bare skin, the elegant curves of her calves, the softness of her thighs. Shoving the transparent skirts up and up as he went.

And when she boldly tilted her hips toward him, heat blasted through him.

Yes. He would give her what she demanded.

His hands reached the swell of her buttocks and he wrapped them firmly around the backs of her thighs, his fingertips tingling with the barest touch of heat from her core. With his thumbs, he held the black lace above her exposed mound. Gold curls glistened, shielding paradise.

Her thigh muscles tightened and Erik glanced up the length of her lush body. Her head was thrown back, but her eyes—heavy-lidded and bright—gazed down at him.

"More teasing?" she asked. Her tone was sultry and thick. Needful.

He smiled. "Not teasing. Savoring. I've been wanting to taste you, claim you, pleasure you with my mouth for an eternity. Now that I've got you where I want you, do not expect me to rush the experience."

She made a short sound as her hips undulated in his hands. "Your patience is unbelievably frustrating."

Erik chuckled thickly and turned his head to press a kiss to her inner thigh. "You'll be grateful for it by the end of the night."

"But it's already nearly dawn. The night is almost over."

"Not here. Not in our world," he murmured as he pressed another kiss to her trembling thigh, slightly higher. "The night has just begun."

The sound she made was an otherworldly growl. "If you don't put your tongue to me right n—"

Her voice caught harshly in her throat before sliding into a moan as Erik covered her clitoris with his open mouth in a hot, suckling kiss. Her hips gave an involuntary jerk but he lifted one of her legs to rest over his shoulder, opening her body for the full attention of his mouth.

Holy hell. The first long glide of his tongue along her honied cleft made his head spin with the musky taste of her arousal. Liquid gold. Fire and sin.

With one hand still gripping her thigh, he brought his other hand between them to gently part her folds, exposing her further to his gaze and the full thrust of his tongue. He wanted to get as deeply inside her as he could go while burying his nose in her soft, sweet-scented curls. When she rocked against him, he softened his tongue and lapped along the full length of her swollen folds before circling her clitoris with skillful, urging intent. He suckled the bud before nipping at her sensitive inner lips then thrust again into her honied center.

The taste of her pleasure wet his lips and soon dripped down his chin.

He couldn't get enough. His body responded to every little sound she made, every tilt and twist of her pelvis, ever delicate flutter and pulse of her flesh. He'd become hard as stone from head to toe, but still he couldn't stop attending to her. Not until she offered that first precious orgasm to his mouth.

And when she finally did, it was glorious.

Her thighs tightened around his head, locking him in place. One of her hands fell to the back of his head and her body tensed with the rushing climax that claimed her.

Erik didn't stop thrusting and licking and sucking even as her hips bucked wildly and her fingernails dug into his scalp.

It was everything he wanted. Complete abandon. Violent pleasure. Passionate surrender.

Once the wave swept through her, it left her shaking and trembling in his hands.

Rising to his feet, he swept her up and laid her on the silk-covered mattress before swiftly divesting of his own clothing. By the time he stepped back to the bed, she'd rolled to her stomach and lifted herself to rest on her elbows.

The glitter of her green gaze greedily soaked up the sight of his naked body.

Erik had always taken good care of himself, enjoying the strength and ability he experienced when he maintained a well-honed physique. It was a welcome by-product that his trim, muscled form pleased his lovers. One he'd never been so grateful for as he was when her hot, desirous gaze settled on his standing cock and she issued a sultry moan of pleasure before murmuring, "Your turn."

Chapter Ten

The man was a goddamned masterpiece. Not to mention a genius with his tongue.

But of course he was. She'd seen the knowledge in his eyes at their first meeting. A man only came by that kind of self-assurance through honest means. And thank God for it!

Her body still trembled with receding pleasure. But if Maxwell was a genius, she was a savant because she knew they'd only exposed the tip of what was to come tonight.

At the moment, however, she couldn't take her eyes off him. His body was honed with muscle. Solid and strong, yet trim and devoid of any unnecessary bulk. Most importantly, so was his cock. Long and thick without being of an obscene size, it curved proudly up toward his belly with a slight tilt to the right. The imperfection made her mouth water.

He stepped toward her at the same time she reached out for him, wrapping her fingers tightly around the base. Hot, hard, satiny flesh throbbed in her hand. She breathed deeply and evenly through her nose, reveling in the pure male scent of him. Clean, earthy, grounding. Then she flicked her gaze upward. Past his taut, rippled stomach. Over his defined chest covered in a sprinkling of iron-gray hair. To the tense line of his jaw, the firm press of his fabulous lips, and finally, to the sharp spear-like focus of his gaze.

Only then did she lean forward to lash her tongue over the head of his cock.

He tensed but said nothing. His eyes held hers with manacle strength and his hands fisted at his sides.

She extended her tongue again. This time executing a more intricate dance around the crown, teasing the slit and the sensitive ridge with quick flicks. He pulsed in her grip, growing even larger. Harder. In reward, she ran her tongue up his full length from base to tip. Then did it again, adjusting the pressure of her tongue, adding a few swirls and delicate little kisses along the way.

Yet still, her teasing did not break his calm or his patience.

Hmm.

Shifting position, she brought her knees up beneath her, resting her buttocks back on her heels. This allowed her a bit more leverage and freed her other hand, which she immediately put to use, cupping his balls as she directed his head between her lips. When her lips slipped past the glans to the veined shaft, he finally issued a deep-throated groan of pleasure.

Sliding her mouth back to the tip, she looked up at him again.

His eyes had closed and his head had dropped back. But only for a moment. Bringing his attention back to her, he slid a hand into her hair to grasp her head with wide-spread fingers.

Yes. This was what she wanted. This show of command. This display of base, primitive need. Her belly swirled with desire and wet heat pooled in her cunny.

For just a second, she resisted his subtle urging, holding her mouth an inch distance from his pulsing tip.

His stomach muscles released and contracted on a harsh and ragged breath as he waited.

But he waited.

Power surged through her. Power and pleasure and something else.

Despite the sexual hunger of his body, the obvious need coursing through him to culminate in the member grasped tightly in her hand, he waited. With his gaze glinting and sharp. His lips pulled back just enough to show the edge of teeth and his breath unsteady. He waited.

And Callista teased.

A quick flick of her tongue to the underside of his pulsing head. A gentle squeeze of his balls. A look of challenge.

To her surprise and delight, he smiled down at her. "Wicked woman," he accused in a gravelly murmur.

She smiled back, but not for long as she was already bringing him back to her mouth. This time, when she took him as deep as she could then slid her mouth back to the crown, she didn't stop. Continuing the rhythm of deep, sucking strokes, she reveled in the tightening of his hand in her hair, the low groans rolling through his chest, and the trembling she began to feel in his hard thighs.

Though she enjoyed this act more than some women, she'd never particularly loved the culmination. But this time, with him, she found herself craving that moment when he'd reach climax and release his pleasure into the heat of her mouth. So much that the thought of him pulsing between her lips had her moaning softly as more heat flooded her sex.

While she lowered her head to tickle one of his testicles with her tongue, he reached over her, sliding his hand down the arch of her spine. He first squeezed one buttock before gently slapping the other. Then he slid his finger down the cleft between, until he reached the flesh that ached so sweetly.

Her moan was full and sultry around his cock as he spread her moisture along her folds before taking her clitoris in a spine-tingling pinch.

Her breath caught and held at the burst of sensations he caused. Her belly clenched with a harsh, hollow feeling. And as she sucked hard on his length in an instinctive urge to fill that void, he eased two fingers deep into her body.

Her exhale was another moan. Involuntary and raw.

He withdrew his fingers then thrust them into her again.

She arched, tipping her hips higher, spreading her thighs, giving more. Demanding more.

He set a rhythm to match the one she executed with her mouth and hands on his cock.

But soon it got to be too much for both of them. In unspoken accord, they shifted position. Erik climbed onto the bed, kneeling as Callista rose up to her hands and knees, turning her back to him.

There was a brief pause as he grasped her hips in his hands.

His erection bumped against her heated flesh, but he did not thrust forward. She glanced over her shoulder as he slid his hands up along her rib cage to her shoulders. There he gathered the full mass of her hair in one fist, twining its length around his wrist.

Then very gently he pulled her up to her knees until her back was flush to his chest. She tipped her chin up and turned her head to the side. He met her there with an open-mouthed kiss that made her bones melt. Their tongues tangled and their teeth nipped.

Wrapping his other arm snug around her waist, he held her against him as he scooped his hips and entered her in a smooth upward thrust. The sharp angle had him hitting all the right spots inside her, making her gasp and shudder. Another short, rolling thrust nudged his head along that sensitive inner flesh that made her thighs tighten and her low back bow.

Again and again, he thrust like that, while his mouth fell to her shoulder. He sealed his lips over the muscle there, sucking hard on her flesh, giving her the edge of his teeth and a hard pinch on her nipple as she gasped and strained and shook in his hold.

A fucking genius. No denying it.

And when he shifted his hold to grasp her breast, her body convulsed, on the verge of another climax. This one promising to be more intense than the last.

His growl at her ear made her tremble from head to toe, her body weakened by the sound of his possession. Bringing a hand up to rest around her throat, he deepened his thrusts and whispered darkly against her skin, "Come for me, Callista. Now."

And she did. The pulsing pleasure overwhelming her like a tidal wave, washing through her, obliterating thought or resistance of any kind.

She'd never been with someone who so effortlessly took command of her body and her pleasure. Anyone who'd tried in the past had been efficiently and subtly redirected. No one had ever seemed to know exactly what she needed before she did herself. No one had ever touched her with such confident and focused intention.

But Erik did it effortlessly.

He was utterly attuned to her shifting needs as she was to his, she realized as they once again changed positions without having to speak. And as she looked down at him stretched out on the black silk while she straddled his lean hips and took him into her still throbbing body, she realized something else. Something that touched deep inside her.

Connection.

The acknowledgement was startling.

As she should have expected, he seemed to sense her sudden disquiet. While his stiff member throbbed inside her, he gently slid his hands up her spread thighs. Then he reached up with one hand to curl his fingers around her nape and pull her down to him. His gray eyes were dark and focused as he brought her mouth to his.

But he didn't kiss her. He just held her there like that as she stretched atop his solid form, her lips hovering a breath from his, his cock buried in her pleasure-swollen heat.

And something pulled taut in her chest. It was a painful, breath-stealing force.

Her first instinct was to become angry at the intrusive emotion and her body tensed. But he wouldn't let her retreat. Instead, he tickled his fingertips across her nape in a soothing caress while his other hand grasped firmly to her rear.

When he spoke, it was in a ragged whisper, words that soaked through her skin and snaked through her blood. "You know what this is, Callista. The truth is evident in your gorgeous eyes."

A hard thread woven deeply into her being would have had her pulling away or scoffing some denial, but the rest of her trembled on the verge of accepting something impossible.

His eyes darkened even more. "Embrace it. Revel in it."

Before she could reply, he pulled her mouth to his. The taste of him ignited red-hot flames in her belly. The swirl of his tongue erased any further thought. The power of his kiss claimed her as his.

Astonishingly, she allowed it.

She sunk into it and surrendered to it. But only for a moment. The feeling quickly grew too heavy, too consuming. The pull in her chest ached. She could not succumb completely, could not give herself over to whatever magic he'd conjured between them.

This was simple lust. An act of physical desire manifested. This was fucking and she knew fucking.

Pushing against his chest, she sat upright astride him and shook her hair out behind her as she rolled her hips to initiate a deeper, more intent rhythm. Sensation sparked and spread out to her fingers and toes. Closing her eyes, she focused on the pleasure, ignoring all else. There was nothing different about this experience than any other before. The man beneath her might be exceptionally—phenomenally!—skilled as a lover, but that was all this was.

Yet when he smoothed his hands up and down her thighs before kneading her hips with his strong fingers as a rough sound of pleasure sounded in his throat, she couldn't keep herself from glancing down at him again.

His body was drawn taut and his head was thrown back. The cords of muscles in his throat stood out and his arms bulged with strain as he held her hips in his large splayed hands. Pleasure had nearly consumed him. He was perilously close to the edge. A few quick snaps of her hips, a squeeze of her inner muscles, perhaps a teasing pinch of his nipples or a bite on his shoulder and he would fall apart.

As she braced herself to finish him off, a dull regret spread through her chest. She wasn't ready for it to end.

In her brief moment of hesitation, he opened his eyes. A fiercely lit gaze met hers and she suddenly felt as though he could see straight through to the darkest pit inside her. He saw it and claimed it in an instant as he sat up and rolled them both over.

In a breath, she was on her back. His cock remained deep inside her as he settled between her thighs. Reaching for her hands, he held them to the mattress beside her head. She lifted her knees, expecting him to start a fast, punishing rhythm to claim his release. Instead, he stilled completely.

The only movement was their chests expanding and contracting with their deep and even breaths.

"You think this is over?" he asked, circling his pelvis in a subtle motion that sent tingling sparks through her core. She bit her lip to hold back the gasp rising in her throat. He smiled. Wicked. Knowing.

Too knowing.

She felt exposed and vulnerable in a way she had never known. And she'd experienced helplessness a hundred ways in her life. It was a feeling she abhorred and spent a great deal of effort avoiding at all costs. Yet this man managed to invoke this unprecedented emotion with a smile.

She might have hated him a little bit in that moment.

"I think you've proven your abilities, Mr. Maxwell," she stated as evenly as she could considering how favorably her body was responding to his physical dominance.

His eyes narrowed at her reply. The light in their depths flickered with something dangerous that stalled her breath even though his expression remained calm. And frustratingly patient. "You speak of sexual gratification, madam. Pleasure is easy to come by and fleeting."

As if to prove his point, he circled his hips again—a deeper, lusher movement that ground his pelvic bone against her clitoris and touched on all her pleasure points.

She arched her spine and tried to roll her hips, seeking more. But he held her too securely, his body pinning hers. Only he had freedom of movement.

"This," he continued in a gravelly voice as he gave a short, shallow thrust inside her, "is something far more precious."

Though her heart lurched and her belly twisted, she stared boldly up at him and forced a flippant reply. "This...is fucking."

There was a flicker of disappointment in his eyes, there and gone in a flash. But she saw it—*felt* it. Her next breath was tight as his lips widened slowly into that smile again. The one that said he knew what she was doing and confidently declared her ploy wouldn't work. The one that promised to give her exactly what she wanted even if she couldn't admit what that was.

Lowering his head, he took her mouth in a kiss with that smile still spreading his lips. She felt it, tasted its dark and lovely sweetness, took the promise of it into herself before he murmured heavily against her lips. "If that's what you believe, then fine. Let's fuck."

He shifted his hold on her hands, interlocking his fingers with hers as he straightened his arms to hold himself above her. Bending his knees, he brought them under her thighs, lifting her hips to accept the deep, full strokes of his cock.

Her body ignited with sensation.

Planting her feet on the mattress, she rolled her hips to meet and accept every thrust.

Yes. This was what she wanted. The power of primal mating. The mindless physical hunger. The reckless, personal striving for sexual satisfaction. She arched and writhed. She tensed and bucked and moaned while he brought her higher and higher with every plunge of his body into hers.

Finally, when she neared the peak, felt the crest beginning to break, sensed the imminent approach of an orgasm that promised to destroy her, she met his gaze again.

And knew in an instant—he was right.

Pleasure exploded like a star throughout her being. Reaching every corner, brightening every dark secret she'd ever possessed, bringing the truth into stark, undeniable view.

And through it all—the gasping, trembling, pulsing release—she couldn't look away from him. She was bound by his gaze. Bound by his pleasure when he finally gave himself over to his own climax with a harsh growl that satisfied a deep animalistic craving she hadn't known existed within her.

She saw the spark of power in his eyes. The possession. The truth.

For those long moments while their bodies communicated in a far more succinct and powerful way than words could ever achieve, she did indeed revel in the beauty of it all.

But feelings so intense and powerful cannot last forever.

Eventually, the trembling slowed, sweat dried, heart rates returned to normal, and Callista's chest tightened with the press of undeniable reality.

She might have experienced something that far surpassed every expectation or understanding of what was possible, but now it was over. The man who'd been so generous and perfect might still be pressing soft kisses to her eyelids, the corners of her mouth, the pulse at the base of her throat, while his member remained hot inside her. But soon, he'd roll from the bed, perhaps mutter a quick *thank you*, and then leave.

Though she'd been pleasured beyond prior experience and had gotten exactly what she'd wanted out of her one night with the man, she wanted more. A hell of a lot more.

But she was no fool. She allowed herself just one more moment. One moment to acknowledge the loss filling her heart. One moment to remind herself who she was and how she'd gotten where she was now.

Men were a distraction at best, a liability and a source of destruction at worst. And Erik Maxwell had just proven himself to be the most dangerous of all.

His hands gently framed her face while his thumb brushed across her lower lip.

"Callista."

Her name was spoken softly but intently in his rich, gravelly voice. She barely noticed his accent anymore, but she heard it then in the way he formed the vowels of her name.

With her belly swirling, she opened her eyes and forced a gentle smirk to her lips. "Well done, Mr. Maxwell."

His gaze narrowed as one brow arched in question. "You cannot bring yourself to call me Erik?"

She lifted a hand to pat the side of his face where black and gray stubble roughened his skin. It took all of her willpower not to caress the hard line of his jaw or drift her fingertips across his frowning mouth. "Of course...Erik." His name felt too perfect in her mouth—succinct, formed with a smooth roll of the tongue that ended with a short kick in the back of the throat. "I suppose I shall have to offer my concession."

"I don't want a damned concession," he said slowly. Heavily.

She tensed beneath him. "Then what do you want? You never did name your prize should the seduction succeed."

Eyes that had been dark and mysterious in the aftermath of his pleasure suddenly hardened. "I want *you*, Callista. Don't pretend you don't know that."

Though a fist clenched tight around her heart, Callista kept a smile on her lips. Sliding out from underneath him, she rose from the bed. "You just had me, darling."

She walked across the room to the washstand. Though she tried to avoid his reflection in the mirror above it, the image of him sitting strong and proud at the edge of the bed, his hair delightfully mussed, his feet planted wide and firm on the floor, his gaze burning a hole in her back, would forever be imprinted in her mind.

She took her time wetting the cloth before smoothing it over her body, wiping away the lovely smell of him. Of her. Of the two of them together.

"Callista, I..."

She really couldn't allow him to go on. The tone of his voice already suggested what he might say, and if she heard him say the words, she might actually want to believe it. And then she'd be doomed for certain.

"I must get back to my guests. You can dress in the other room if you'd like. I imagine you can find your way out."

The silence that followed her words was as cold as any winter she'd endured in her poverty-stricken youth.

It was best if he decided to hate her.

They could go on in their prospective business endeavors, never having to cross paths again. If he happened to see her in the street or at the theater, he could avoid her with a scowl of disgust and eventually she wouldn't even be bothered by it.

"That's it, then?" he asked thickly.

Lifting her hands to twist her hair up into something resembling a proper coiffure, she replied, "What else could there possibly be?"

He didn't reply. And after a while, she risked glancing in the reflection at the room behind her.

It was empty. He'd left.

Chapter Eleven

"Hiya, Lissy." Mason sauntered into Callista's personal study. It was a rare occasion her brother visited Pendragon's these days now that he had a family to care for and protect. But when he did, it was always unexpected and usually at the worst possible time.

Today was no exception. It was the morning after her grandest party of the year...the morning after her night with Erik Maxwell...

Though she'd changed into a slightly more comfortable day gown, she hadn't slept yet and her mood was growing more atrocious by the minute.

"What the hell do you want, Mace?"

Her brother's expression was one of false shock and insult. "Can't a man visit his only sister for no reason?"

"Not you," she snapped.

He grinned. Settling his overly large, muscled frame into one of the chairs facing her desk, he tilted his head and arched his brows. "What's the matter? You're particularly prickly today."

"It was a long night."

"Right! The event of the year. Not the success you'd hoped?"

"It was a crush," she replied flatly. "Early estimates suggest it was the most profitable night in Pendragon's history."

"Hmm."

She didn't like it when Mason made that sound. It meant he was thinking. And that was never a good thing. Whenever he used that clever brain of his, he ended up saying something she didn't want to hear.

"It's that Maxwell bloke, isn't it?"

Dammit.

Something in her expression must have confirmed his assumption since Mason burst into laughter. It was a rich and hearty sound that warmed her despite herself.

He'd had too little cause for laughter as a boy. She'd been born twelve years before her little half brother, and though she'd tried to shield him from the worst of their shared father, she hadn't always succeeded. And then she'd been forced to leave. Eventually, she managed to get Mason out of the hovel they'd come from, but she'd always wished she could have done more in his youngest years.

But now he had Katherine. And Claire and Freddie. Her brother was doing all right.

Some might suggest he was doing even better than she was herself.

Rising from her seat behind the desk, she wandered across the room. It was a foolish attempt at avoiding the conversation looming ahead of her. Foolish because Mason was not likely to let the topic die.

And because a part of her actually *wanted* to talk about the man who'd been haunting her thoughts since he'd risen from her bed.

"Talk to me."

Looking over her shoulder, she noted her brother's stern countenance and the shadow of concern in his green eyes, just a couple shades darker than her own.

For so long, he'd been the only person she'd truly cared about.

Of course, she cared for the women who came under her protection, but in the way of benefactor, guardian, and mentor. Her feelings for Mason were different. He was her only family. Her blood. Looking at him now and seeing his protective, supportive demeanor, she had to admit that although she'd helped him in a myriad of ways, she had never been very good at showing him what he meant to her.

Her chest ached with the acknowledgement. Damn, but she was terrible at this emotional shite.

Mason rose to his feet and rolled his head atop his broad shoulders. "Do I need to go have a talk with the arsehole?"

She rolled her eyes. "No." The next breath she took caused the ache in her chest to tighten rather painfully. "But I might be long overdue for one."

He appeared startled for a moment before he stepped forward, his hands rising as if to offer an embrace. But then he recalled himself and lowered his hands to his sides. "What's this about, Lissy?"

Meeting her brother's intent gaze, she felt a prickling pressure behind her eyes she hadn't known in decades. "I fucked up, Mace."

It was almost comical how Mason looked at her, as though she'd suddenly become a different person. And in a way...she had. "What'd you do?" he asked, his tone slightly incredulous, slightly wary.

"I chased him away."

"So, get him back."

She scoffed. "It's not that easy."

"Sure, it is," he argued. "You want the man?"

Want him? *Yes.*

And more.

With a rough sound of frustration, she whipped her skirts aside and crossed the room. "What's the blasted point? It cannot last. Nothing like that ever does. It's a fool's illusion."

"So, be a fool. Take the bloody risk. It's fucking worth it, Lissy."

Keeping her back to her brother, she shook her head. She'd avoided that kind of risk all her life. Starting with her own mother, Callista had seen far too many times what a woman's love got her—beaten, sold, degraded, lost to the desires and demons of men.

Of course, she'd also encountered men who were noble and honorable. But as a whole, they were rare creatures. Despite his rough edges and crude demeanor, Mason was one.

And Erik. He was one.

But that didn't guarantee a thing.

"Listen," Mason said behind her, setting a hand on her shoulder to turn her back to face him. His brows were furrowed and his gaze met hers with surprising compassion. "Whatever this is, you've gotta play it through to the end. And if he turns out to be an arsehole...or if *you* end up being the arsehole, you deal with that when it comes. Sometimes it doesn't work out." His eyes darkened and she suspected he was thinking of Claire's mother. But then his mouth tilted in an irreverent grin. "But when it does, Lissy, it's pretty fucking amazing. Don't cheat yourself out of that possibility just because you're a little scared."

Callista narrowed her eyes at that last comment, which he'd obviously added just to provoke her. Mason knew damn well she was not afraid of anything.

But then again... *Was* fear holding her back?

The answer hit her like a fist to her sternum. Dammit to everlasting hell. That wouldn't do at all.

Giving Mason a look that would turn most men to stone, she noted in a dangerous voice, "You know what? I'm pretty sure *you're* the arsehole."

He threw his head back and laughed. "That and more, as my duchess would no doubt attest."

"I don't know how that woman puts up with you."

His smile then was full of pure male arrogance. "The lady loves me." He lifted his fists and curled both arms to flex his biceps. "And these. She fucking adores these."

With another roll of her eyes, she turned and walked away. "You know the way out," she offered over her shoulder as she continued from the room, his laughter echoing behind her.

MAXWELL'S BUTLER GREETED her at the door with a shallow bow and a sweep of his arm toward the stairs. "You'll find him in his sitting room, madam."

She'd suspected on her last visit that Erik had given instruction to allow her free entrance, but now she was sure of it. Why hadn't he rescinded the order after last night? She would have if their situations had been reversed. She honestly never would have wanted to see his face again if he'd treated her the way she'd treated him.

Heat flowed across her nape and her low belly twisted. This was going to be harder than anything she'd ever done.

Though a hollow feeling settled in her chest—she refused to call it fear—she made her way up the stairs to the concealed doorway.

During that first visit, she'd guessed his reason for so readily revealing the secret passage to his private rooms was to demonstrate his consideration of her—the great Madam Pendragon— as a business colleague. A professional equal. Having his butler lead her through the secret passage to his private rooms hadn't been a careless choice. She knew him well enough now to be assured that Erik Maxwell did nothing carelessly. At the time, she thought it a clever if presumptuous move. Madam Pendragon had no equal and she'd been anxious to enlighten him on that basic fact.

But now, as she triggered the latch to open the panel, a new understanding dawned.

She'd come to Maxwell's nearly a fortnight ago, prepared to stand toe to toe with him, to threaten him if necessary. He'd been yet another man who endangered her business, her very livelihood, and most importantly, her power.

She had consistently ignored his assurances to the contrary and construed nearly everything he did as a manipulation to get what he wanted from her.

And what was that exactly? What had he wanted?

Just her.

He didn't need her power and influence. Nor her wealth. Nor her clients.

He wanted her. And blast it all—she wanted him as well.

Her steps lengthened with purpose as she headed toward the room where they'd shared the bottle of brandy. Striding through the open door, she saw him standing before the fireplace, staring into the flames. He was still in his evening wear from the night before though he wore no coat or cravat and his sleeves had been rolled back to his elbows.

A combination of hope and fear churned inside her. It was a new sensation, something she wasn't entirely certain she was prepared to experience. But she was here now and she refused to be a coward. Setting her shoulders and lifting her chin, she started across the room, her skirts making a soft sound as they swished about her legs.

Alerted to her presence, he glanced over his shoulder. Surprise flashed briefly in his eyes before he turned to face her, putting the fire behind him and his face in shadow. He did not speak as she approached and neither did she.

When she stopped in front of him, he squared his shoulders and removed his spectacles. She was close enough now to see his face, to look into his eyes. Close enough to draw in his familiar scent. Close enough to desire his touch.

She steeled herself against the wanting. She'd come here intending to confess her feelings, but first, there was something she needed to understand. Titling her head, she tried to keep her expression as neutral as his as she looked up into his shadowed gray eyes. But an unfamiliar fire burned inside her. A fire she was struggling to contain.

After a moment, he spoke, his voice quiet but strong. "I didn't expect to see you today."

Callista made a dismissive gesture before replying, "I assure you; I didn't expect to come here."

He lowered his chin and met her fierce gaze with one of calm intensity. "Then why did you?"

"Before I answer that, I'd like you to explain something to me. And I'd like you to be completely honest."

"Always." The single word rang true and poignant through her being.

"What was your true intention when you offered to seduce me?"

The corner of his lips twitched. "Getting you into bed was not a proper enough motivation?"

Callista smiled in return. A practiced, knowing smile. "Of course it is. If it's the only one."

There was a pause. Then his voice was thoughtful as he replied, "I'm prepared to answer you in full honesty. But it won't matter if you're unwilling to accept the truth."

She narrowed her gaze, daring him with a hint of danger in her eyes. "Try me."

Another twitch of his lips. "From the moment you appeared in the doorway to my office, I knew something remarkable had just entered my world. I was undeniably intrigued by your cunning mind and bewitching manner. I was determined to know you better."

"Do you feel you accomplished that goal?" She arched a brow imperiously. "Do you know me, Mr. Maxwell?"

His silver-gray eyes sparked from beneath a furrowed brow. "I know your success was hard-won and that your business is much more to you than financial security. I know you have a hard time acknowledging that, despite your strength and influence, you still experience loneliness. I know you prefer to lead the way in your personal relationships and I suspect it's because you've been disappointed in the past. People have taken from you—or have tried to," he corrected with a tilt to his lips.

Lifting his hand, he traced his fingertips across her temple as he swept a tendril of hair behind her ear while his gaze remained locked with hers.

"You are clever and crafty beyond anyone's understanding. You've hardened your heart to protect it and you do not believe in love because you've witnessed how the emotion can be falsified and manipulated." His focus dipped to her mouth and his words thickened as he added, "Your lips taste like heavenly sin, your skin is softer than silk, and your moans of pleasure twist me into knots."

Callista parted her lips as something intense began to snake through her, stirring up emotions she struggled to identify. She wanted to refute his claims but his words rang too true. Every one of them.

His gaze lifted to hers again as the flat of his thumb gently brushed over her cheek. "But there is still so much I want to know about you. I want to know how you take your tea or if you prefer coffee. I want to know how your eyes look upon waking. I want to know what amuses you and what infuriates you. I want to discuss your hopes and dreams and fears over breakfast every morning and talk to you about the weather and the latest town gossip every evening."

She didn't realize she'd begun to shake her head until his hand slid away from her face. His expression darkened as a furrow of disappointment clouded his brow. "You don't believe me," he stated in a low voice.

That was the problem. She *did* believe him.

She didn't know what to think of everything he'd just said, but she couldn't deny how she felt about it. Elated. Terrified. Hopeful.

Turning away, she crossed to the windows, where heavy drapes blocked out the light of day. She pulled one of the drapes aside to gaze over the white and wintery scene. Carriages rolled along the snow-covered street as people bustled about, bundled in furs and wool. So mundane. So domestic.

For so long, her world had been contained within the walls of Pendragon's.

Mason dared her to take a risk.

But how did one go about risking their very heart?

She felt his presence as he silently came up behind her. "I don't know how to do this," she murmured quietly.

"Yes, you do," he assured.

Letting the curtain fall back into place, she turned around. His gaze met hers and within them she saw a quiet conviction, calm confidence, and heated longing. His lips were pressed into a firm line, but it didn't stop her from hungering for them. And suddenly, kissing him was all she could think about.

That, at least, she knew how to do.

Slipping her gloved hand around his neck, she pressed her body to his as she rose up to place her mouth against his.

Though she wished he would, he didn't encircle her waist with his arms or pull her in tighter. He stood there, patiently accepting whatever she was willing to give, leaving it up to her to push it further.

And just like that, in a flash of certainty, her fear was gone.

Wrapping both arms around his neck, she deepened the kiss. With passionate intent, she slid her tongue along his then drew his lush bottom lip between her teeth. Finally, his arms came around her and the satisfaction of being held secure in his embrace filled her with warmth and desire.

Pulling back just enough to murmur against his lips as she looked into his lovely eyes, she said, "I know you didn't want a concession, but I'm giving it to you anyway. *You've got me.*" His eyes blazed and she smiled. "Now what are you going to do with me?"

He answered by shifting his hold to sweep her up into his arms before heading toward the door. "Now," he replied with sensual intent, "I'm going to make love to you until we are both so exhausted we fall asleep with limbs sprawled and sweat cooling on our skin. And when we wake up, we'll start again and again and again."

Her laugh was husky with anticipation. "And then?"

At the end of the hall, they entered a large bedroom decorated in jeweled tones of sapphire and emerald. He carried her straight to the bed, where he followed her down to the mattress. Settling atop her, he took her face in his hands. His voice was rough and low as he answered her question in a thick murmur. "I'm going to devote myself to convincing you that love is real and wonderful and yours for the taking."

Callista's heart thundered in her chest, and as she looked into his intense gray eyes, she realized she'd be a fool to deny the truth shining from their depths.

And Callista was no fool.

Don't miss out!

Visit the website below and you can sign up to receive emails whenever Amy Sandas publishes a new book. There's no charge and no obligation.

https://books2read.com/r/B-A-PMBH-EHJLB

BOOKS 2 READ

Connecting independent readers to independent writers.

Did you love *The Secrets He Keeps*? Then you should read *Noble Scoundrel*[1] by Amy Sandas!

To protect a daring young lady and her brother, he must defeat his villainous past or lose the only thing worth fighting for.

Hardened by a childhood in the rookery and honed by years as a bare-knuckle boxer, Mason Hale revels in his reputation as a ruthless moneylender to London's Underworld. But everything changes when he commits to caring for his young daughter and the mysterious boy who protected her when Mason couldn't.

When Lady Katherine Blackwell discovers someone is intent upon abducting her brother for an unknown purpose, she has no one to turn to except a man known for brutal efficiency in the boxing ring and on

---

1. https://books2read.com/u/m2ZpMG

2. https://books2read.com/u/m2ZpMG

the streets. She just needs Hale to keep her brother out of danger while she uncovers who is behind the attacks.

As the East End scoundrel takes up residence in their Mayfair manor, Katherine starts to suspect their bodyguard is made of more than brute strength and a brash attitude. And though Mason has no illusions regarding his sordid and violent history, the more Lady Katherine declares she doesn't need a hero, the more he wants to be exactly that.

If you like shameless heroes, intrepid heroines, and undeniable chemistry, you'll love Amy Sandas's bold new historical romance novel, Noble Scoundrel.

Read more at amysandas.com.

Also by Amy Sandas

Peril & Persuasion
Noble Scoundrel
The Secrets He Keeps

Reformed Rakes Novella
Wicked
Dangerous
Brazen

Regency Rogues
Rogue Countess
Reckless Viscount
Rebel Marquess
Relentless Lord

Standalone
Kiss Me, Macrae
Reformed Rakes Box Set

Watch for more at amysandas.com.

About the Author

Amy grew up in a small dairy town in northern Wisconsin and after earning a Liberal Arts degree from the University of Minnesota – Twin Cities, she eventually made her way back to Wisconsin (though to a slightly larger town) and lives there with her husband and three children. She spends her early mornings writing before heading off to her day job. The rest of her time is spent trying to keep up with the kids and squeeze in some stolen moments with her husband.

Read more at amysandas.com.

Manufactured by Amazon.ca
Bolton, ON